Ron Mueller

Border Crosser

Books and Stories by Ron Mueller

Fiction Series
The Alex Evercrest Series
The River Front
The Girl on The Grill
Missing
Maggot
Racist
Votive Candles
Windy City
Country Road
Pool of Blood
Sins of the Daughter
Body Parts
The Skull Collector
The Vanishing
The Shadow Fighter
Moonshine
Grief's Trajectory
The Magic Touch
Northern Lights
Alex Evercrest Heroine
Alex Evercrest Collection Two
New Direction
A Family Affair
Disruption
Aftermath
The St. Lebuinnus Church Murder

A Brian O'Neil Novel
Hawaiian Phoenix
Moon Curser
Death Broker

The Problem Solver Series
Solutions
Drug Lords
Border Crosser
The Problem Solver Collection

The Taelo Series
The Early Years
The Golden Feather
Journey of Discovery
Dangerous Passage
Condor Clan Slingers
Circumvention
The Journey of Sages
Collection
Future Leaders Journey

A Taelo Story:
White Swan and Quiet Pheasant
The Child's Name
Floating Cloud
Quiet Rabbit
Busy Bee
Little Otter & Talking Wren
Broken Spear
Burley Bear & Meadow Flower
Taelo Story Collection

Science Fiction

The Savitar Series:
Journey's End
Savitar
Confluence
Savitar Series Collection

Bram Nielson Series
The Fold
The Message
Fold Wormhole
Negative Fold
Ripples in Time
Bram Nielson Collection

Single Science Fiction Books:
Current Past and Future
The Event
The Door
Viajante 7

The Problem Solver: Book 3

∎ Border Crosser ∎

Ron Mueller

Around the World Publishing LLC
Cincinnati, Ohio 45242

This book is a work of fiction. Names, characters, places, and incidents either are products of the author's imagination or are used fictitiously. Any resemblance to actual events or locales or persons, living or dead, is entirely coincidental.

Border Crossers ©

ISBN 13: 978-168223-174-6

Distributed by Ingram
Cover Picture by Bruce Rolff @Dreamstime
Cover Design by Ron Mueller

Ron Mueller

<u>Dedication</u>

To all the people

seeking a better life

in the best country in the world

Ron Mueller

<u>Introduction</u>

It is a troubled world.

The human species has, like no other, risen to dominate the world. The rise is marked with amazing beauty and grace.

It is also marked by cruelty to other humans and a disregard for the negative impact they have on their only home, the Earth.

The beauty found in poetry and writing, the beauty found in paintings and sculptures is more than countered by the wars, the intentional environmental destruction, and the barriers each separate country imposes on its peoples and the neighboring states.

The belief of limited resources, the behavior of greed, the desire for wealth and the desire for control are all factors in the behavior exhibited by those who surface at the top of the heap. The ability of various leaders, in a myriad of areas, to convince those more interested in their immediate family well-being allows those interested in domination to rise to positions of influence and power.

Often their belief is that they have been ordained to be in charge or alternately they are smarter and should be in the lead.

The rise of the rule of law has created a situation where fairness is managed by laws developed by the representatives of the people. Even in the situation found in the United States that has three branches of government designed to maintain the system of fairness to all, slavery, and women's right to vote were initially missed. More recently the rights of gay or lesbian people are in question.

Human greed, cruelty, misbehavior, and disregard of the environment seems to increase asymptotically with the rapid rise of the population.

Justice is not always served. This situation is managed by a secret organization that funds and directs the actions of The Problem Solver. This is a person whose principles, judgement, behavior, and actions guide him in how to resolve problems that otherwise would be left unchecked.

The problems are many. The problems are anywhere in the world. The problems are solved in the best manner that The Problem Solver determines.

Introduction

See if you agree with the problem resolutions, that this Problem Solver, Ian Sinclair, has chosen for his various assignments

1 Border Crossers

*I*t was pitch black, the screaming, the crying, the pounding, the sound of bone shattering and the ungodly scraping of bone against steel reach Marial's ears. She held her six-year-old daughter's and her nine-year-old son's heads against her chest and prayed. She asked forgiveness for her sins as she took her last few breaths.

Her life in Guatemala had been hard and she had lost her husband when the rebels came into her village and raped her. He had defended her only to have his head cut off by a machete.

Her two children had been out playing and had survived.

She had chosen to try to escape the horror. The long road up through Mexico had been hard but she thought of it as the road to a place where there was hope. A place where she and the children would find peace. A place where they would grow and prosper.

She had traded the one small treasure, two ounces of gold that she and her husband had saved. It was their dream to leave their village. They had talked about making the journey to the promised land.

When she crossed the Rio Grande, she felt a surge of hope. When she ran and got into the back of the large white van, she felt a surge of hope. Hope continued to carry her as in the pitch black the van ran for hours. Then the van shuttered to a stop and hope began to ebb and was slowly replaced by fear and then fear was replaced by despair.

She sat quietly in the dark singing softly with her children in her arms. In the pitch black, her dreams were replaced with the nightmare she was now living through. She was sure that the nightmare had only one ending. It was an ending that she had never envisioned. She felt each of her children stop breathing. She knew she was next and once again asked for the forgiveness of her sins.

Ian watched as the news camera zoomed in on the back of a panel truck. It had been found by the Arizona highway patrol abandoned in the scorching hot Arizona sun. The external temperature had reached an ungodly one hundred thirteen degrees.

The truck was filled with more than thirty bodies. It was clear by how they were piled up trying to scale the interior wall of the panel truck that the occupants had used their hands or a boot trying to break out.

Ian was sure that to the end the occupants were desperately shouting, crying, and pleading to be let out. The backdoor was bent, and one occupant had broken his leg, and the bone was exposed in a grotesque angle. The hands with their fingernails ripped back clearly indicated to Ian the final desperate efforts to claw their way out.

Ian absorbed the scene as the camera pulled to a distant view and then zoomed in on a mother cradling a young girl and boy to her chest. The three seemed to be in a Cinderella sleep just waiting to wake up.

The reporter walked away with a cloth over his nose as he commented about the stench of death. Some bodies were already beginning to bloat. There seemed to be an even mix of men, women, and children. It was clear to Ian that this had been mostly family units trying to get into the US.

The woman holding her children to her chest became the focus of the reporting. The report was picked up by all the national news channels and it went viral on the personal chat sites. The picture went viral with multimillions of hits in just one evening.

Ian let out a groan when he heard a national news caster say, "We need action to be taken against those trafficking in across the border people smuggling. We especially need someone to take action against smugglers that abandon people in locked trailers. This has got to be fixed." This Ian knew was clearly a message for him to act. He was the problem-solver.

Ian watched several other major channels and listened to the same message, saw the same iconic picture of the mother holding her two children to her chest. There was no doubt. The message could not have been clearer.

Ian left the grand family room. It was the place where he spent each early morning with a cup coffee and listened to Morning Joe before tuning in on BBC, CNN and then going on to Fox. He liked to keep a balanced perspective on what was being watched by the rest of the world. So much of what was presented as news was actually biased opinion by one side of the political aisle or the other. The worst of the group seemed to be Fox

Ian went down the hallway to his study.

He walked in and took in the book lined shelves along the two side walls of what had originally been a large spacious home library but over the years had become his office. The mahogany desk with a black three-foot-wide all in one computer faced the rear window overlooking the tennis court and the lawn around it. The Library was where he spent many hours doing research.

Ian booted up the computer and began his search on the topic of smuggling people.

After a moment he opened the bottom left hand desk drawer and extracted a locked box from the very back. He opened and picked up an older phone that did not have GPS as a function. He slowly dialed a well memorized number. It was immediately answered. By the tone of the voice, he was sure the person on the phone had been expecting the call.

"Send me everything you have on smuggling people across the Mexican border. Set me up as an FBI agent with orders to go to Arizona. Give me the name of the current field agents name that manages that area. Arrange for me to get there in two days. And thank you," Ian said as politely as possible.

Early in his career as the problem-solver he had tried to be friendly, but he was soon calibrated on the fact that the people on the other end of the line were to remain anonymous.

Whoever they were and however many made up his support team was unknown to him. He had envisioned a large work area all full of people doing his bidding and he had also envisioned a gray-haired old lady with coke bottle bifocals sitting in a darkened closet like office. He would probably never know which of the two scenes was the closest. All he cared about was that his support team always delivered what he needed. His support team showed up in the field in various ways that helped him but once again he never directly saw any of them.

The requested material began coming in almost immediately. They must have anticipated his request. He reviewed the information from past reports on the smuggling and movement of those coming across the border. It was very thorough and detailed.

He learned of an earlier abandoned truck full of people. It had not made the news.

The fact that two trucks had been abandoned in the last two months seemed to indicate carelessness, disregard or perhaps it was the result of an increased pressure by local law enforcement that frightened the drivers and caused them to abandon their trucks.

Smugglers always preferred to remain anonymous. Getting caught was one of their greatest fear. Subsequent publicity meant exposure and scrutiny which meant that their bosses were as likely to kill them as anyone.

The US border patrol preferred to keep the media at arms-length which meant they whenever possible kept their actions and findings under wraps.

Inadvertently this penchant to keep press coverage low caused the police to aid the smugglers.

Ian looked up the local law enforcement officers in Phoenix. Phoenix was where the Highway Patrol, the Local county sheriff and the FBI regional offices were located.

He reviewed the background and assignments of the local FBI Phoenix office chief. He seemed to have a well-rounded background including a stint in the Army. He appeared to be a solid individual with personal integrity.

The human smugglers had to get past the security, monitoring and patrolling done by Homeland Security. In fact, the border patrol units of the Homeland Security organization were highly trained and highly motivated. Ian's assessment was that they were good at their jobs.

He also suspected that some of them must play some part of the smuggling operation. The crossers had to get past the field teams and that indicated some sort internal agents working for the cartels. These agents most likely were bribed and receiving some sort of monthly amount of money.

The local sheriffs and State Highway Patrol seemed to be vigilant in their efforts to intercept the cars and trucks involved in the smuggling. They seemed to focus on looking for those being smuggled. It was unlikely that they had any direct involvement, but he would at this point not rule it out.

Ian suspected that there were a few bad actors in these organizations that would cause the good side to get a black eye. He was certain that there was one or more bad apple in the local law enforcement agencies.

He listed the ways people could be crossing the border and not be getting caught.

There could be participation by local law enforcement personnel. There could be a group of border guards that would look the other way. In all cases it appeared that those doing the smuggling had help on the US side of the border. Help that with the right incentive would let the smuggler get the people seeking to get into the United States get past the border security.

Ian knew he needed to go to the field and get firsthand knowledge to understand the true situation.

He had already asked for his FBI persona to be reactivated. He was Herman A. Lunquist, senior FBI investigator.

Ian reviewed his past history as Herman. It had continued to be updated and he laughed about some to the more current compliments and his work performance evaluations. Someone on his support team was having a good time fabricating and building his history.

He had many personalities on record but only a few got reactivated as often as Herman had been. For his Journey into the Heart of Russia, he had become a naturalist. In taking care of the Three Bad Pennies in the Gaza, he had become a cameraman.

This was a natural build because he had taken on the role of a cameraman on a team of National Geographic photographers out to document the Elephant Ivory trade plight. For fighting the Pirates off the coast of Africa he had become a sailboat captain.

Ian let Lesley know that he had an upcoming business trip out west. She immediately knew what kind of business and as always gave him a kiss on the cheek and told him to be careful. Over the years Lesley had come to accept the fact that Ian would remain a problem-solver for most of his life. She constantly reminded him that they had the small fortune most people dreamed of having and that they did not need the money.

Ian gave her a hug and thanked her for loving him.

Herman Lundquist had a high status as an FBI agent. He called Mike Lancaster the local FBI branch manager, introduced himself and let him know that he was coming to do some field work in his domain. Mike had agreed to meet him at the airport and escort him to the local FBI office.

As he came to the end of the airport concourse and walked out of the security area Ian spotted Mike almost immediately. Mike was roughly six two with dark hair that was cut almost in a short military style. Ian put him in the handsome category. He smiled as he thought that in his dark suit he could have starred in the movie, Men in Black.

Ian could tell that Mike was nervous and probably wondering why he, a senior FBI investigator, was there. In the car on the way to the office Ian explained that he had been sent to work with him because the FBI hierarchy was feeling pressure about the fact that two loads of people had died in the back of trucks and there seemed to be no solution in stopping it.

Mike thanked Ian for clarifying his presence and that he could see the reason he had been sent. He wondered what Ian was going to do.

Ian admitted that initially he planned to get a lay of the land and see if anything popped up that would help him determine what he could possibly do that had not been done so far.

The FBI office was in the local Federal building in the heart of downtown Phoenix.

On their way up from the basement parking lot, Mike informed Ian that an office had been arranged for him and that they would share Mary Gems as their secretarial support.

They approached Mary's desk where Mike introduced Herman Lundquist.

After some small talk and asking about her family, Herman asked if she would set up breakfast or lunch meetings with the leaders of the Highway Patrol, the Sheriff's office, and the Homeland Security Leader.

Herman made the point that he wanted his meetings to be on an informal basis. He did not want formality to become a barrier. He wanted everyone to know him on a more personal basis and feel somewhat relaxed around him.

Mary agreed to do so but made the point that the Homeland Security Leader was located in a small town about two hours away.

He suggested that meeting be arranged to meet the Homeland Security Leader's timing.

Mike next led Herman to an office next to his.

Herman commented that he hoped not to be at the desk at all.

Next Mike walked to a small room with a coffee pot, a shelf full of cups, a small refrigerator and stainless-steel sink.

"This is as good as it gets here in the office. If you want something better, May's restaurant just down the street makes a great breakfast and lunch and serves a variety of soft drinks, iced tea as well as great cup of coffee," Mike fired off in rapid order.

Herman could tell that Mike was still nervous.

He had a good feeling about Mike. He could see them working well together.

Herman followed Mike out of the coffee room

He asked Mike to bring him up to date on the investigation of the deaths of the people found in both of the abandoned panel trucks.

Mike said that the trucks were registered to two separate local truck rental companies. The rental companies had contracts on file for the trucks and everything was in order. The persons renting the trucks and their driver license information were fake. The information on both rentals led nowhere.

The FBI was working with the state and states around to see if they could determine who the drivers might have been. The trail at this moment was cold.

The records of the companies were being reviewed to determine how many other times a truck had been rented under a fictitious name. The net had been cast wider and truck rentals from all rental companies were being scrutinized.

Mike commented that it would take time to get through this investigation.

Herman commented on the impressive and solid approach Mike was pursuing. He went on to describe how great it would be if the two of them solved this current case and put an end to trucks being abandoned.

He asked Mike to speculate what action he would take if he could take any action he wanted. What would he do?

There was a soft knock on the door just as Mike was about to answer. Mary opened the door and informed them that she had set up breakfasts for the next three days for the two of them.

Herman thanked Mary and she closed the door.

He then suggested that he and Mike continue their discussion over lunch.

Mike led the way to May's. He said that he recommended the Reuben special.

After lunch Mike dropped him off at the downtown hotel.

Ian checked in and went up to his room. After a long shower, he sat down and turned on his computer and thoroughly reviewed the information he had on each of the law enforcement leaders.

Mathew Martin was the leader of the highway patrol. In his mid-fifties Mathew had served in the Marines. He had a wife and three children, all now in their late teens and early twenties. He had an impressive record and had quickly risen in the state's highway patrol organization. It made no sense to Ian that he would be involved.

Bill Peters was the local sheriff. He too had the same family profile. He had an Army background and had been elected sheriff four times. He was known for his active participation in getting downtown Phoenix renovated and well-lit, so people could safely enjoy their time in the city.

It made no sense to Ian that either these two would be involved.

He, however, did not rule out the fact that someone high in their organization might be involved.

The next morning, he walked to May's diner. The appealing smell of fresh rolls, bacon and was trumped by the smell of coffee. As the waitress poured his coffee it immediately captured Ian's mind and made his stomach growl. He sat down and looked around. He had arrived early, so he could watch the customers come in.

Someone in a dark blue city police uniform with a gold badge on the chest came in and sat in a far corner booth. A moment later a person in a tan uniform with State Highway Patrol embroidered where the sleeves met the shoulder came in and joined the person in the corner. They both looked over at Ian.

Ian took in the two seasoned, well-aged older men sitting in full uniform at the booth. He stood and walked over and introduced himself as Herman Lunquist. He had planned to meet first with the highway patrol leader, but it was clear they had talked to each other. The Highway Patrol leader introduced himself as Mathew Martin and then introduced the City Police Chief, Bill Peters.

Mathew said he preferred to be called Matt, said that the two had talked and decided that they would meet the investigating FBI leader together.

Herman thanked them for having breakfast with him.

At that moment Mike walked in and came over to the table. He apologized for being late.

Ian noted that Mike seemed to be treated as one of them.

Herman was the odd one out and was the one they all seemed to be wondering about. He surprised the group by asking about their families and the age of their kids. He had the statistics of each family, but he was interested in listening to how each of the people at the table related to their family.

The discussion that followed made it clear to him that "Matt" and Bill were old and good friends. He made note that these were family men, proud of their work and solid in their integrity. This made it easier for Ian. If there was corruption in their organization, it would involve those below these two. The problem would be deeper in the organization, but he would not be fighting the organization leaders.

After breakfast, Ian accompanied by Mike went on tour of the border and to the office of border security to see how they operated.

The drive to the office of border security took over an hour. Ian used this time to get to know Mike. He listened as Mike described coaching his two sons in soccer, baseball, and basketball. Mike did not want his sons to play football because of his own experience and the injuries that were only getting worse with age.

They arrived at the Homeland Security office and met with Ricard Butterfield the regional director. Rick, as he wanted to be called, showed Herman a map and the way the area was patrolled. He invited Herman on a drive through tour along the border.

Herman gladly accepted. Rick led the way to a large, air-conditioned trail buggy and for the rest of the day he, Mike and Rick drove the route that his border guards patrolled.

It didn't take Ian long to figure out that the guys in the field needed directions from the drones that flew overhead.

They and their dogs made great teams. The dog handlers all took to Herman once their dogs allowed him to scratch them behind their ears. Their dogs showed them that Herman was OK. They commented that Herman was one of a handful of people that the dogs accepted.

Ian laughed and replied that his wife thought he was a dog too.

The team described how they went about their normal daily patrol. Their manner was professional, thorough, and very conscientious.

After learning about how the field teams were guided, Ian asked to tour the drone control office and understand how they interacted with the ground team.

Rick said the tour would need to be the next day around noon. He was joining Matt and Joe for his usual midweek breakfast at May's. He asked whether Mike would be there.

Mike answered in the affirmative and looked at Ian to see what his response would be.

Herman answered that he wouldn't miss it.

The next day after breakfast Mike and Ian followed Rick back to the Border Patrol offices. Rick led the way in and walked Ian and Mike through the normal observation shift and the communication with the border patrol vehicle surveillance and the dog patrol teams.

It was clear the drone handlers had the best vantage point to see almost everything. A mole on this team could easily provide the information that would misdirect those on the ground.

On the drive back, Ian asked Mike to check on the background of all the drone operators.

Ian again guided the conversation to Mike and his family.

Mike described his home as strategically located between the Middle School, where his youngest son and middle daughter attended, and the High school where his oldest son was now in his junior year.

The family church was just beyond the middle school. The family doctor was located across from the High School and a hospital was just a stone's throw north of the high school.

He and his wife belonged to a health club less than three miles away. Mike described it as a convenient arrangement for the entire family.

He had a large two story, five-bedroom home on a corner lot that faced third street and was blessed with a dead-end street to its right. That meant a quiet back yard and a street with almost no traffic on one side.

Mike made a point of mentioning the nine-foot interior ceilings of the house that kept the air conditioning bill reasonable. He liked the fact that the large size of the house and the relatively small size of the lot made the yard work reasonably easy and the entire package affordable.

Mike extended an invitation to Ian to a family grill out. He explained the grilling would happen out in the backyard, but because of the heat everyone would be taking shelter in the air-conditioned back patio.

Ian said he would love to meet his family and looked forward to the grill out.

Ian spent Saturday sleeping in late, taking a swim and working out. He took in a movie and spent some time reviewing the case.

Sunday morning early Ian took a walk-through downtown Phoenix. The heat of the day was building when he flagged down one of the few cabs and gave him Mike's address. He sat back and enjoyed the short ride out.

The grill out and meeting the family put Ian in a good mood. Then toward the end of the day Mike received a call. He beckoned Ian over and quietly shared the fact that the border patrol had lost a large group of border crossers but had seen a light grey or perhaps dirty white panel truck leaving the area.

Ian and Mike agreed to meet early before going to and figure out what to do before going to breakfast.

That evening Ian began to study the routes that he would choose if he were transporting illegal aliens and wanted to minimize his chances of getting caught. Based on the mileage of each of the two confiscated trucks that had been previously used Ian plotted various routes. He decided to check these routes with Matt and Bill at breakfast on Monday morning.

Ian met Mike at the office and suggested that they have breakfast at Mays. He had questions for both Bill and Matt.

Mike was especially interested in Ian's study on possible travel routes and wondered why his team had not done something similar.

Ian pointed out that he had no clue about travel in the region, but he didn't know what else to do so he was doing what he always did best. He created his own sandbox to play in and hoped there was no cat shit in it.

There seemed to be one route that best fit the miles. It also ended just shy of Interstate 40, which was a main East-West traffic corridor. Ian had used a red pen to trace Highway 80 north, to 75, to 78, to 180 then on to 32, 36 and finally 117. This brought both trucks very close to Interstate 40. It was a slow tedious route, but it certainly kept the trucks off the main thoroughfares.

Ian figured that it was probably around this area where a transfer to other modes of transport would be made. There could be may second leg routes depending on the mode of transportation that had been arranged. There were endless dispersal scenarios that Ian could think of.

Matt and Bill concurred on the route Herman liked best. They figured it was as good as any and asked what good knowing this would now do for those who had died.

Herman agreed that it did nothing for them, but he felt it might help to be ready for the next time. And he pointed out that Rick had let Mike know on Sunday that a white panel truck had left the border.

Ian decided to drive and feel out the route he had mapped. He figured his chances were very low of finding anything, but the drive would occupy him and give him time to decide on the next steps he needed to take.

He asked Mike if the office kept any cases of water handy and found out that indeed they had extra cases on hand. He asked that several cases be put in the trunk.

Mike said he would have one of his guys put it in the back of the car Ian was being issued and asked if Ian was expecting to find a truck load of people.

Ian replied that he had no clue, but he was going to be Boy Scout ready.

Ian walked out to the assigned car, checked the trunk, and threw in his small personal needs bag.

Ian left Phoenix and began what he decided was a scenic drive through the scraggly pine covered mountains surrounded by a wide skirt of sage, cactus and tumble weed stretch of barren desert. Ian encountered almost no traffic. An occasional car or truck going the opposite direction broke the otherwise monotonous drive.

He was thinking through what he had learned so far and almost missed what he was looking for. He was almost all the way to Interstate 40 when a white panel truck stopped on the side of the road caught his eye. He slowed down as he drove past.

He saw no one.

The truck seemed to be deserted. A red flag went up in Ian's shocked mind. Unbelievably it was the exact scenario he had imagined.

Ian decided to go back to the truck and take a closer look. He parked just past the truck on the opposite side of the road and carefully approached the truck. He looked out to the right of the truck to see if the driver was out in that direction. The underside of the truck was clear. It seemed the truck was deserted.

It was just not possible went through his mind.

He walked up to the cab and stepped up on the sideboard to look inside.

Almost immediately there was pounding on the panels from inside the back of the truck. He walked to the back of the truck. The doors were locked.

Ian pounded on the backdoor and in Spanish he told them to wait a moment. He would open the back doors.

The truck had a cross lug nut wrench but no straight bar. Ian went to his car and came back with the hockey stick style lug wrench most cars carried. The lock was a standard case quarter inch shank. It snapped on his first hard twist.

A swoosh of hot air from inside hit him as the doors came open. Ian was almost overwhelmed by the smell of sweat and urine. He was immediately angered by these conditions. The relief of finding everyone alive was the only thing that placated Ian. He helped those inside get out.

The people needed help and they needed water. Ian knew that his earlier premonition that caused him to ask for the two cases of water now confirmed why he was still alive today. He always seemed to have these premonitions.

Ian passed the water out and told everyone to drink slowly so they would not be sick.

He got everyone out and had them sit in the shade of the truck.

Ian saw a white van approaching slowly from the direction of Interstate 40. He took a bottle of water and went to the front of the panel truck. He stood leaning against the front of the truck. The heat of the radiator hitting his back added to the heat of the sun. He could feel the beads of sweat forming on his forehead.

The oncoming van stopped about twenty feet from the truck. Two men with guns drawn got out and approached him.

They asked what the hell Ian was doing letting the people out of the truck.

Ian calmly told them to take it easy and that he had stopped to see if he could help. Ian pointed to the engine compartment. He told them that he was a mechanic in Phoenix and just happened to be driving back from a job he had just finished. Ian went on to claim that he had fixed hundreds of engines of this type and that he could help them.

The taller of the two said they would fix their own truck and Ian should just get on his way.

Ian took note that the group along the side of the truck were now standing and quietly watching. The presence of the group seemed to distract the two gunmen.

The two had finally reached the distance when Ian could go into action. He waited until the two took their next step forward.

The taller of the two took the step forward that Ian had been waiting for. Ian threw his water bottle at him and took a long step forward. He deflected the gun hand with his left hand while at the same time stepping down hard on the arch of his right foot. He kept the gunman's body between him and his partner. The final stiff finger stab to his throat took him down.

As the taller gunman was just beginning to crumble, Ian delivered a round house kick to the second gunman's temple area and followed it with a downward fist blow to his nose. The second gunman fell down on his knees holding his nose with two hands and then toppled over. Both gunmen were out.

Ian quickly picked up the two guns and checked the two for any other weapons. Both were carrying large hunting style knives.

Ian threw the knifes back into the on-looking crowd.

He asked the on lookers to take off the men's boots and pants and to throw them both into the back of the truck.

Ian was surprised by the energy and enthusiasm the crowd displayed as they picked the two up and took off the articles Ian had specified. They literally threw them into back of the truck. There was a cheer when the doors were shut. It was clear that the two had earned the displeasure of the people they had left locked in the truck.

Ian would interrogate the two but first he had to disperse the people that were now looking to him for guidance.

2 Imelda

Elisa lay against her mother's side. She was hot and thirsty. She and her mother had been riding in the absolute black darkness in the back of a truck for a very long time.

The truck started jerking and then stopped.

When they had first jumped into the truck Elisa had been happy because they had escaped the patrol dogs. Her friends had told her the dogs ripped people apart and ate them. But now she was hot, thirsty, and really scared. She could not even see her mother's face, and the air smelled really bad. She kept her head on her mother's chest and listened to her mother's heartbeat. Her mother kept praying and singing, which really worried Elisa.

Imelda hugged her daughter. The heat was unbearable. They had not been given any water or provisions. She and the others in the group that were in the truck with her had crossed the border into the US during the night.

They had come through a hole cut in a fence as the guide brought them across the river and then they had jogged for about a half mile to where the truck was waiting for them.

Imelda When she picked up Imelda so the two of them would not be left behind, she had dropped her bag with all her valuables. They had all jumped into the back of the truck and the doors were shut. It was hot, and the ride was bumpy and bruising until they reached what must have been the highway. Then it was a long monotonous ride in the pitch-black interior of the truck.

The heat and the bad smell seemed to go up simultaneously. She hugged Elisa to her chest and said a quite prayer.

She was on the way to meet her husband in Cincinnati, Ohio. He told her he had a small place to live and was working for the state as a gardener in a local state hospital. They had agreed it was time for her to bring Elisa and come live with him.

Now as she sat in the back of the truck she wondered if their lives back in Oaxaca had been all that bad. Carlos and she had been friends since they were kids. Their families lived on adjacent small farms and did fairly well. They grew most of their own food and raised a few goats and sheep. Their chickens provided eggs and meat.

It was a simple life. It was a good life for a poor family. But it held little hope that the future would be any different than the past.

The two had married shortly after getting out of high school. Carlos went to work for a local building materials supplier. He got his pay partly in goods and a small amount in cash.

He got permission from both of their families to build a small home on the boundary property where the two farms came together.

Carlos and Imelda had sketched out a small single story two-bedroom home. A tiled entry hall split the home with one bedroom on each side. The bathroom and shower were on the left back corner. The kitchen was the biggest room in the house and featured a large table at its center. A window over the sink looked out to the outdoor cooking area.

Every day Carlos would bring home a few bricks or bags of cement. Every weekend the two would work at building the next part of their home. It took them almost a year to build their home. The two had worked together every evening. This was a fond memory for Imelda. They had grown closer together with each brick they cemented into the wall. Each was a gold brick that strengthened their love for each other.

There was a big party to celebrate the completion of the home. They moved in and immediately they felt a new surge of hope for the future. Imelda became pregnant only a few weeks later. Her pregnancy was another cause for celebration.

The next big event was the drilling of the well and then having electricity brought to the house. Each was followed by celebration.

Life was good.

Elisa was born in December. Dark brown eyes, a full head of black hair, blessed with all her fingers and toes, she was a perfect child. It was the most joyous of times. She was their Christmas baby.

Carlos was a consummate father. Always good with his work roughened but skilled hands, he made a crib by hand for Elisa and a rocking chair for her. Both were treasures Imelda cherished.

For a few years, their lives seemed to be going smoothly and making progress.

Then the economy went bad. Carlos lost his job. No matter how hard he tried he could not find another.

He was despondent and had a feeling of hopelessness. Their few chickens and small garden kept them from going hungry but there was no income and they had little money in reserve. Carlos was despondent and shared his feeling of hopelessness.

A friend of Carlos told him about working in the US and how several of his friends were up north and sending money home to their families. The jobs were not hard to get and if one lived economically the money was enough to send home and to save.

Shortly afterwards Carlos made up his mind to cross the border to the US. His friend's friend lived in Cincinnati and vouched that there were abundant jobs to be had.

Carlos experienced an easy trip. His crossing went smoothly, and he quickly made his way to Cincinnati. Once he arrived, he called back home and told Imelda how easy it had been. Only the border crossing itself had been somewhat challenging and scary, but the rest of the trip was no different than taking a trip into Mexico City. His calls and a few letters shared the various part time jobs of gardening or working on small construction projects. The money he sent home was more than enough for Imelda to live on and to provide some extras for Elisa.

Life on the farm was again good but Carlos was missing.

When he landed a permanent job, he asked her to come to Cincinnati. He felt the US offered a better chance for their family to get ahead. Elisa would get a good education and have the chance to go to college. Carlos was thinking ahead about what was good for his family.

Imelda shared her decision to go to Cincinnati with both sets of grandparents.

At first both grandparents asked her not to go. They understood the bleak future that staying in Mexico meant for Imelda, but they wanted to have their only granddaughter close at hand.

All of them saw how much both Imelda and Elisa missed Carlos and they then became supportive and wished her good luck. Imelda turned down their offer of money and instead left most of what she had saved with her mother.

She and Elisa were now into their second week of travel. Elisa had been especially afraid of the border crossing. They made the crossing with a group of about twenty people made up mostly of young men. Counting herself there were four women in the group. She was the only one with a child.

When border guards seemed to approach them with dogs, their guide told them to run as fast as they could to a white panel truck waiting for them. Imelda had dropped all her belongings, as she scooped up Elisa so she could run and keep up with the rest.

They all jumped into the truck and the doors were closed. The truck lurched forward and went speeding away. It was pitch black in the truck and everyone remained quiet. Someone with a cigarette lighter flicked it on and they all got a quick look around the empty truck. There was no water or food.

Imelda now had a new worry. She had no money, and she did not have a way to get to Cincinnati.

Occasionally there were some whispered conversations. Otherwise, there was only darkness and silence.

Imelda softly hummed some of Elisa's favorite songs. They were together and soon she hoped that somehow, they would get to Cincinnati.

Then the truck sputtered, shuddered, jerked and came to a stop. Everyone got ready to get out, but the doors did not open.

Fear slowly crept into Imelda's mind. She hugged Elisa to her and made a prayer to the Virgin Mary asking that the doors would open.

Someone pounded on the side of the truck. Another group kicked at the backdoor.

Imelda just kept praying.

It seemed they had been still for a very long time when suddenly the truck leaned as if someone was getting into the driver's side of the truck.

Almost everyone began pounding on the side of the truck walls and yelling at the top of their voices.

Imelda just kept repeating, "please open the door."

The rattling of the lock on the back door caused everyone to suddenly become silent.

Then in what Imelda considered the best bad Spanish she had ever heard; someone call out and let them know that he was going to open up the backdoor.

She knew it was not either of the two who had been driving the truck. They were Mexican and spoke perfect Spanish.

Imelda crossed her herself and thanked the Virgin.

As the doors opened, the people in the back rushed out. It was hot out in the sun but there was fresh air to breathe.

Imelda led Elisa out and into the shade that was on the desert side of the truck.

She was surprised to see a total stranger, a gringo, helping them.

She watched as he went to the trunk of the car across the road. He had two young men carry two cases of bottled water across the road.

He took the first two bottles and gave them to her and Elisa.

He kept a third for himself but did not open it.

Imelda had tears in her eyes as she thanked him.

Everything went silent as they heard a van was coming toward the front of the truck.

Imelda watched as the generous man that had opened the door went to the front of the truck. All he had was a bottle of water in his hands.

Two men got out of the truck. Imelda realized they had their guns aimed at the person that had freed her.

This time her prayer was for him.

It seemed that the person she was praying for had no idea about the danger he might be in.

Imelda moved behind the front left wheel of the truck and put Elisa behind her. She listened to what was being said.

Suddenly the man moved so swiftly that she almost missed what was happening. The two men with guns were down, moaning and bleeding. The strange man had both their guns and was asking the two be thrown into the back of the truck. He told the crowd to take of their shoes and pants before locking them in.

She was surprised to hear herself shouting when he asked for some help in throwing the two men into the back of the truck.

Imelda leaped up to help but she was pushed aside by the rush of several of the men. She suddenly realized that she did not like the two men on the ground. She had paid a lot of money and had been treated worse than a pig.

She wanted to give the stranger helping her a hug.

Imelda came back to her bleak reality. She was in trouble. She had no money. No clothes but what she had on. She was hungry, and she had a young daughter who was clinging to her in fear.

Her mind kept returning to one thought, "How was she going to get to Cincinnati? She went from a high at getting out of the back of the truck and getting water to an extreme low despair.

She once again said a prayer.

<u>*3 Deliverance*</u>

*I*an looked down the empty road toward the way he had driven out toward Interstate 40. He turned toward the Interstate and looked at another stretch of road in that direction. It was all empty and going one way as going the other. He had the two culprits locked in the back of the van and thirty or so people standing in the shade of the truck.

The day was coming to its peak temperature. He was sure it was more than one hundred degrees in the shade. The two in the back of the truck would already be feeling the much higher heat inside the truck. Ian would wait a little longer before he interrogated the two. They would be more willing to cooperate after exposure to the stench and to the oven like temperature.

He had to disperse the border crossers. Ian was not interested in turning the group in. He inquired about who could drive the van parked in front of the panel truck. Several hands went up. Ian picked the oldest of the volunteers who he took to be near his thirties to do the driving.

He then asked how many were expecting rides when they got to the interstate. He noted that most of the hands were in the air.

Most notable to Ian was that the women did not raise their hands. The woman with the young girl was hanging her head.

He figured she realized she was in trouble.

Ian inquired about the names of the women and of the young girl. The distress in the mother's voice made it clear to Ian that she needed help.

"I am Imelda, and this is my daughter Elisa. She is turning eight this year," Imelda spoke up. I had bus tickets to go to Cincinnati, but I lost my backpack and all my belongings when we had to run for the truck. The driver of the truck was to take us to the bus stop.

Imelda's plight helped Ian make up his mind.

He told the women they would ride in his car. They should continue standing in the shade until he got the men on their way.

The men all managed to squeeze into the van. It would be a hot ride, but it was only a short distance to the Interstate. The van made a U turn and went back toward the Interstate.

Ian walked back to the car and opened all the windows. He told Imelda to sit in front with Elisa and to relax while he went and asked the two in the back of the truck a few questions.

He walked back to the truck and picked up his tire iron. He walked around to the far side and poked several holes in the side wall.

Ian asked if they were still alive. There was an immediate plea for him to let them out. Ian said that it would continue to get hotter as the sun hit its peak. If they wanted out, they would have to tell him who they worked for.

He was met with silence.

He hit the side of the truck with his tire iron and said goodbye. He wished them a good life for as long as it could last.

Ian heard one of them say it was an official in the highway patrol. They did not have a name.

Ian replied that they would not live very long if he left, and he was leaving if they did not give him a name.

"Wait, Wait, we get our orders to rent a truck and where to go over the internet. We do as instructed. We pick up the border crossers and drive to the designated location. Once the border crossers are on their way, we return the rented truck. Our pay gets transferred into our bank accounts. We never see or talk with anyone.

"How do you know it is a high-ranking official in the Highway patrol," Ian asked.

When we were first recruited the person said that he had the cover of the highway patrol at the highest level.

Ian asked for their email names and wrote them down.

He next asked if they had been the drivers of the truck found with dead people in the back. He expected the denials they gave. He would check there whereabouts later.

Ian quickly verified the email names they had given him.

He then unlatched the door and told them to get out. He told them to walk toward Interstate 40. They were to walk there and disappear from the area.

They asked for their pants and boots.

Ian laughed and said that they had on what they were going to walk in. He had looked around and realized that the clothes had been taken by the men who had left.

As they began the walk the tallest one complained about his broken foot and crushed Adam's apple. The shorter one complained about his broken nose and the lump on the side of his head.

Ian replied that they had met the devil, and they should be happy to be alive and not down burning in hell.

Ian stood and watched them until they were at least a thousand paces down the road.

He put in a call to the Highway patrol to pick up the two men walking toward the interstate in their underwear. He instructed they be taken back to headquarters and held.

He then returned to the car. He started the engine and put the air conditioner on high and closed all the windows. Then he made a U turn and went toward the interstate.

The flashing red lights of multiple highway patrol cars surrounding the van and the men standing in a row with their hands up clearly showed the fate of the men who had driven up in the van.

Ian looked at Imelda and told her that the men would be processed, and many would be allowed to go to their US destinations. Some would be returned across the border.

Ian proceeded on and got onto the Interstate going east.

Imelda asked where Ian was taking all of them?

He replied that it would depend on what they told him. He asked for the names of the people who connected them to the border crossing guides and that they tell him where they were going. He was watching the three in the back. He repeated the question in Spanish.

They all started to talk at the same time.

Ian stopped them and asked Imelda to tell her story first.

Imelda assured Ian that it was not a gangster but a family friend who knew someone who could get her connected with a border crossing guide.

Ian made it clear he was not interested in any family friends. He described the scene of a truck just like theirs but full of people who had died of the heat. They had been discovered only a few weeks back. There was a mother, daughter and son all huddled together. They had died in her arms.

Imelda had tears in her eyes as she hugged Elisa and told him she was on the way to Cincinnati to meet her husband.

Imelda whispered thank you God. She wished she had her rosary.

Ian let her know that he would put her on a bus that would take her to her husband.

Each of the other three gave the names of their contacts in Mexico and where they were planning to go. It surprised Ian to learn that one was going to Minneapolis to meet other family members. One was on the way to Auburn, Maine to live with her best friend. And the last was on the way to Washington, DC where she had been offered a job at a local hotel.

Ian told them what was going to happen. They would spend the night at a nice hotel. They would have a pleasant evening meal at some family restaurant. He would buy each of them bus tickets to their destinations. Tomorrow they would get on their buses and make the remainder of the trip on their own

Imelda asked why he was doing this for them.

Ian explained that he did not always know why he did what he did, but he smiled and said that this time it was because Elisa smiled at him.

It was so true.

Ian never tried to reason why when he made these types of decisions. He figured someday he would either meet the devil or be standing at the pearly gates trying to explain his grievous sins.

Let's stop and get all of you some basic clothes to wear. Imelda, you, and Elisa go into Target and buy two outfits each and some shoes as well. Buy a small suitcase for each of you. And get anything else you need such as toothpaste and toothbrushes. Pay cash Ian said giving her enough money to cover the shopping.

"You three go separately to Sears, Kohl's and Burlington Clothes factory," Ian instructed the other three as he gave them cash as well.

Once they had departed, Ian dialed his support number and requested reservations at the Ambassador Suites, the bus tickets for each of the women and one thousand dollars in cash. He asked that everything be sent to the Hotel.

He did not want to buy the tickets at the bus station because it would make his activities too traceable, and he wanted enough cash to hand out.

Ian also called into the office to let Mike know that he had been on the road driving the routes he suspected the border crossers took. And had intercepted the truck. He let Mike know he would be back by noon the next day and that he wanted to interrogate the drivers of the panel truck.

Imelda and Elisa were the first to return. They walked toward the car pulling their very practical matching dark blue suitcases. They were smiling and talking to each other. It was great to see the two finally relaxed and happy. Elisa was wearing her new "just do it" sneakers.

Ian had a couple of throw away phones in the glove compartment. He took one out and handed it to Imelda. He instructed her to call her husband and let him know that she and Elisa were safe and, on the way home. He told her not to say anything more than that and that once there she could tell him the whole story. He looked at Elisa told her to say hello but told her say anything either.

Ian could hear the happy ring in Carlos's voice as he talked to Imelda and Elisa.

Ian watched as the other three met each other on the sidewalk. They were chattering as they walked back to the car. Each had bought a different color roller board.

Ian stopped at an restaurant for a quick dinner. The endless salad was a hit. Everyone found something on the menu they liked. Elisa especially seemed to like the buttered bread sticks. It was clear that they had all been hungry.

One of the women asked why he was being so kind. Ian replied that sometimes good things happened, and they just needed to accept it and later they should be kind to someone else. He really did not have a good answer but in his mind, he linked his actions to the much darker and deadly actions he often took when solving problems.

Ian told them that they all had room reservations at the Ambassador Suites under names he had given them. They should pay cash. He instructed the three to go first, that they were friends returning from vacation, sharing one room and for the night they were Maria, Eli, and Fran. He told them not to talk too much and that they should just check in, go to the room, enjoy a good shower and catch a movie. He instructed them to stay in their room until morning.

He said that he would check in next.

Imelda and Elisa were to come in last. He said that their names were Angela and Justine and that they were on the way home.

He said they would all have breakfast at seven on the ground floor and told them to their evening.

Ian moved the car to a parking space and got out, took his overnight case that he carried in the trunk and headed for the lobby.

Imelda and Elisa were on the sidewalk coming in slowly behind him.

A shower and a cup of coffee, the evening news and he was ready for bed. Ian called home and talked with Lesley and let her know all was well. Hearing her voice and listening to her tell him about her day put him at ease.

The next morning, they all met for breakfast on the first floor.

Ian had already checked out. The clerk had handed him a grey envelope that had been dropped off for him. The bus tickets and money were inside.

The five looked totally refreshed and quite local in their new clothes. It was clear by their consumption that they really enjoyed their breakfast. Ian could tell Elisa was having the time of her life.

He knew that years later she would remember only the good part of her journey and would have to think hard about how frightened she had been only a few hours earlier.

Imelda was quiet. She was so relieved to be safe. She still found it strange to get the help that she was getting from a stranger. Her prayers had been answered.

He made sure everyone had checked out. They all enjoyed a long morning breakfast. Ian then led the way to the car. There he handed each their tickets and ten twenty-dollar bills. Elisa got her own ticket and her own ten twenty-dollar bills.

Each said gracias and asked how they could pay him back.

Ian told them that there was no way to pay him back but that someday they would be able to do something good for someone else. When that happened, they should do it. He told them that doing so would make them feel very good about themselves.

He knew it made him feel that way.

As she got out of the car at the bus station, Elisa asked if she could write to him.

Ian would be living in the same city, but he knew that it would not be safe for him to stay in contact with her. He lied and told her that he would keep in touch with her and gave her a hug.

He got back in his car and began his drive back to Phoenix. He was going to find out if there had been someone in the highway patrol office involved by the fact he would know by finding the two drivers alive.

4 The Devil and the Drivers

I

an took the same route back as the one he had taken out from Phoenix. The white panel truck was gone. He had expected it to be.

As the miles clicked over, Ian was more certain of a high probability that there was a connection in one of the law enforcement agencies. He pondered how he might determine who that person might be.

He came to the conclusion that there needed to be a connection or helper in the border patrol organization. He was more confident in finding that person. His focus area was on the drone monitoring team. He thought that person might need help to coordinate their actions.

Ian arrived at the federal building and parked his car in the basement next to all the other non-descript government vehicles.

He decided first to find out what had happened to the group of people he had helped and then were caught at Interstate 40.

The sergeant on duty at the highway patrol desk looked at his computer screen and let him know that they had been sent to homeland security for the normal entrance processing. Each would have their day in court.

The sergeant went on to let Ian know that two of the people picked up were still in the holding cell. He chuckled and said that they had been picked up walking barefoot and only in their briefs. They had admitted to driving the panel truck that had hauled the border crossers away from the border. They wanted a lawyer and were threatening to sue because they claimed some policeman beat them up. They were in a sorry state and their feet were bleeding when they were picked up. He went on to share that they were to be transferred to the city jail because the city had jurisdiction since the two lived here in Phoenix. The police would be picking them up sometime in the afternoon.

Ian asked the sergeant not to let the transfer happen until he heard from captain Martin.

He let the sergeant know that he planned to return immediately afterwards meeting with the captain to talk with the two being held.

The sergeant told him good luck on getting them to talk. They have refused to talk until they got a lawyer.

Ian had doubted the two in the holding cell about some high-ranking official in the highway patrol being the leader. When Ian learned of the transfer to the city police a red flag went up.

The fact that the two had survived the night in highway patrol custody immediately transferred his suspicion as to where the higher contact resided to the city police.

He went to May's restaurant to get some coffee.

He approached Mathew's support, Marilyn, with her favorite

cup of latte from May's and handed it to her as he walked past her and told her he had to talk to the boss.

She informed him that she was supposed to stop him but made no move to do so but instead took a sip of her latte and raised one eyebrow and said thanks. She knew she was not going to stop Herman.

Herman handed an angry looking Matt a cup of May's plain black coffee as he excused himself on the phone and hung up.

What the hell, I told Marilyn to keep everyone out. Then he stopped.

"Thanks, I suppose you bribed your way in with a latte for Marilyn. What's up?" Matt said as he took his coffee. He was surprised that he was getting to like Herman.

Ian apologized for his disruption but came right to the point that someone in the Phoenix police department was involved in managing the transport of the border crossers.

He went on to explain that the Highway Patrol had the two drivers of the transport in a holding cell. They were scheduled to be picked up by someone from the police department in the afternoon.

Ian then put forward the theory that the two would never reach the city jail alive but would be killed during their escape attempt.

Matt made the comment that he had just started to like him and now he came in with this story.

He wanted to know how Ian could possibly have gotten such information since his department had tried to question the two and had gotten nothing from them.

He went on to say that Ian did not seem to be such a trusting person that the two would just volunteer the information to him.

Ian gave a small laugh. He shared the fact that he had locked the two up in the back of the panel truck and threatened to keep them there until they cooked to death. It was hot enough that they gave him just enough information. He had then released them.

Your men picked them up along the road soon after. You saw and treated their condition. That was also my doing.

Matt simply said Oh! That explains their police brutality claim.

"So how do you figure it is somebody high up in the Phoenix police department and not someone in the Highway Patrol. Why not me," Matt inquired?

"Well, the two in the holding cell informed me that someone, high up in the Highway Patrol department had hired them. Since they are still alive today, I figured it wasn't you or anyone in your organization," Ian said with a smile.

"What if they had died during the night," Matt asked?

Herman smiled and said that then instead of bringing coffee he would have entered to arrest him.

Matt chuckled and commented that the coffee tasted even better.

Ian pointed out that the two in the holding cell had no clue as to the actual person or persons who hired them might be. They got their orders and their pay via the internet. They could easily have been misdirected on purpose.

"What kind of help are you asking for," Mathew inquired?

"I want the two men to wear a wire and I want your department to follow the city police transport and listen in on the conversation that goes on during transport."

Matt first defended Bill, the chief of police. And said that there was no way he would be involved and do such a thing. He did not need money and had grandchildren that he spent all his free time with. Matt said he thought that the idea was crazy.

Ian replied that he did not think it was Bill but asked that he be kept out of the loop in the near term. He was sure that the culprit had to be someone Bill trusted. Ian pointed out that they would know almost immediately if there was someone in the sheriff's office and at breakfast tomorrow Ian would personally apologize to Bill if he was wrong.

Matt said he would support him, but he did not think that the two in custody would agree to wear a wire. If they did wear a wire and made it safely to the city jail, he would have hell to pay with Bill.

Ian agreed and again said he would put himself in front of that train if he was wrong. He said he would not have asked if he did not believe he was right.

Matt was under the impression that the two would not agree to wear a wire. They have been stonewalling ever since they arrived, and insisted they wanted a lawyer.

Ian replied that he would convince them to wear a wire. And asked that Matt call Mike and have him come over.

Ian walked back downstairs to the desk sergeant. He asked to be taken to the holding cell.

The desk sergeant stopped in amazement as the two inside the cell jumped up and stood up at attention. He looked at Ian and commented that there was something about him that these two respected. The two had so far refused to stand because the condition of their feet.

Ian approached the cell and simply said hello. He asked about their claim that they had been mistreated. He asked if there was some complaint, they would like to share with him?

They both shook their head to indicate no. The strained look on their faces almost made him laugh.

The sergeant commented that the two had been a pain when the highway patrol tried to question them. They had refused to even talk. You say hello and they immediately stand at attention.

Ian had made a point of learning the sergeant's name. He now let Bob know that he needed a few moments alone with the two. He asked for about ten minutes. After that the folks who would outfit the two with wires should come in to do so.

Bob commented that it was a little unusual but said that if he needed anything he should just press the buzzer on the wall.

Ian told the two in the cell to sit down and listen. He asked them if they knew that they were being transferred to the city jail. They said they had been told that.

Ian asked if they believed they would live to see the inside of the sheriff's jail cell.

Eduardo, the tall one, asked Ian who he was.

Manuel the shorter one reminded him that than Ian claimed to be the devil.

Ian replied that he certainly was willing to play the part of the devil but in their case, he was trying to save their lives. He pointed out that he was interested in the person or persons at the top of the ladder that paid them.

He told them they would be dead by late in afternoon if they did not cooperate. Whoever the people in the police department may be, they will kill you as you try to escape.

Eduardo asked why they would try to escape. They had received good treatment so far.

Ian told them they would be taken somewhere to the edge of the city and told to go home. After they stepped out of the police van, they would be shot in the back with the cover story that they were trying to escape.

Ian let the silence stand. Then he stood and reached for the buzzer, and he told them good luck getting to heaven.

Manuel asked what they needed to do.

Ian informed them that they needed to wear a hidden microphone so he could hear what the men picking them up were saying. He said he expected those transporting them would probably be friendly and tell the two that they were going to be dropped off outside the city limits. They would be instructed to go home, get their stuff and to move on. They will tell you they will send instructions to you later. Or they will tell you some other similar story. However, when they let you out of the police van, they will shout out "stop" and as you run or turn around to look at them, they will shoot you.

How do you know this Eduardo asked?

Ian replied he would do something similar if he were the person in the police department managing the operation.

Eduardo then said they would cooperate. He wanted to know how Ian would help them afterwards.

Ian replied that they would be held accountable for their deeds, and they faced up to thirty years in jail, however he would make sure they got the best possible deal for their cooperation and would probably only get a fraction of that time. He would also recommend a minimum-security prison.

Eduardo looked at Manuel. The two were silent for a moment and then agreed to wear the wire.

Ian gave a nod and let them know that they would soon be outfitted with the microphones.

Ian left the cell as the officers that were there to outfit the two with the wires walked in.

He went to the sergeant and asked where he would take the two if he was planning to kill them and make it look like and escape.

The sergeant gave a good chuckle and smiled. He went on to explain that the scenario that Ian had just described was the talk at almost every beer drinking outing that the local law enforcement held.

One group had the scenario playing out somewhere south of East Dobbins Road out on South Central Avenue. Another group talks about going out on the 303 or the 74 west of I 17. A third group talks about going out on 87 north. He made the point that it was all drink and all talk.

He then made the point that almost any short drive outside the city would do. There were many secluded out of the way places.

The sergeant asked if he had passed the test.

Ian pointed out that looking at the city map he figured the police van should go southeast down North West Grand Avenue. Ian was trying to figure out where it was most likely to go if the police van deviated from that route.

The sergeant put his finger on the map and said he would take them out on that road.

Ian asked the sergeant to make sure that the drivers of the city police van did not know what was going down.

He was pleased to hear the sergeant exclaim that if there were any crooked cops in Phoenix, he wanted them caught and punished.

5 A Short Ride

Ian walked slowly up the stairs. He could hear the coon dogs yelping as they got the scent of their prey. He could see the stars overhead as his gas head lantern lit the way before him. He could feel the adrenaline rush. He was closing in for the kill. His adrenalin level was at its peak.

Ian knew that it was only a matter of time. He realized he did not know how many people worked for Mike. By now Mike should be in Matt's office. Matt had mentioned he would have his team ready to go. Ian needed at least four different cars to follow the police van. He did not want the driver to notice he was being followed.

Matt was sitting with Mike discussing the logistics of moving the various cars along the direction the city police transport van would take. Mike was in control of four cars and the chief said he had as many.

Ian asked Matt to be in charge of positioning the eight vehicles and that he would just be along for the ride. He also requested that the people in all the vehicles be in street clothes.

Matt gave a small laugh. He said the sergeant downstairs figures you are the one in charge of everything that is going down and he said to help or get out of the way.

Ian looked at Matt and Mike. He could see that they too had the adrenaline rush going. He suggested that a quick lunch would help all of them.

During lunch Ian kept the conversation on family and events going on in the city. He wanted to keep the focus away from the coming action.

At three the dark blue van with Phoenix City Police painted on the sides pulled into the State Trooper's pick-up area. The shackled, Edwardo and Manuel were led out and put into the back. As per protocol seat belts were put on before the doors were closed.

Ian watched as the van went down toward North West Grand Avenue. It was headed in the right direction. He wondered if he was wrong.

A few moments later a call came in letting them know that the van had turned off Grand Avenue and was headed south down 19th Avenue.

Ian was listening in on the conversation that was going on in the city police transport van. The conversation with Edwardo and Manuel was almost verbatim to what Ian had told them they would hear.

He was sure the two were now paying very close attention to what was going on.

The transport turned east on West Dobbins. It appeared that Ian would be buying Bob, the sergeant at the desk, a beer. Bob had said that the southern scenario would be the one he would choose.

Ian listened as Matt instructed three of the cars to head south on South Central. He positioned two cars north of the intersection.

The cars tailing the van kept switching so that they would not be discovered.

Matt and Ian were following behind all of them as Matt directed the flow of the cars like a chess master playing in a tournament.

The van made the expected right turn and headed south on South Central avenue.

Matt instructed the three lead cars to go just past where South-Central crossed Phoenix South Mountain Park. He was counting on the fact that the park provided the right conditions for the planned killing.

Matt had all the cars closing in from behind. His car was up front.

Ian continued listening to what was going on in the van. The van drove into a secluded area at the entrance to the park and came to a stop.

The tailing highway patrol vehicles parked, and everyone ran out to surround the city police van. It seemed to him they were generating a hell of a racket. Ian was surprised they had not been discovered.

Ian was standing by a tree directly behind the van. He did not need his headset to hear Eduardo and Manuel being told to get out and find their way home.

Ian heard the escape call going into the city police dispatch office. The two transport policemen were just raising their guns to fire when he stepped out and shouted that they were under arrest and for them to put their guns down.

The two foolishly turned and fired at him. He took one bullet in the chest, but the other shot missed. He knelt and returned fire. He was sure they were wearing bullet proof vests like himself, so he shot each of them in the leg to get them down.

Since he was sure they were wearing bullet proof vests like himself, he shot both of them in the chest. He wanted them alive, but he wanted them to feel the pain he was going to feel from the bullet that had hit him.

Matt and Mike rushed over to Ian. They were amazed that the forty-five-slug embedded in the vest had not knocked him down.

They were more amazed that Ian had taken down the other two in such a fashion that they would live to be prosecuted.

Ian knew he would have a large chest bruise accompanied by an ache once the adrenalin rush subsided but at the moment his adrenaline was covering any pain.

Mike took over the scene. An ambulance was on the way to take the two wounded policemen to the hospital. He assigned two of his agents to stand guard over the two policemen going to the hospital. They were instructed to only let himself, Matt, or Ian in.

Ian asked to have a word alone with the two he had shot.

Ian walked over to the two who were still laying on the ground. He let them know that he knew they had help back in the city police department. They needed to make a choice to save their skin or get the maximum time of around thirty years for shooting an FBI agent and they would get the maximum time for being accessories to the death of thirty people in the back of the van discovered a few weeks ago.

Ian waited for a count of thirty. OK, keep quiet, it's your funeral. I am sure those above you will make sure you never get to talk. They will transfer your money in the offshore bank accounts to their own and freeze you out. Then they will make sure you never get to trial.

Ian watched the surprised look on their faces. It had just occurred to them that they might be killed.

Ian was standing to leave when he was asked about the deal. They would give him information for a good deal.

Ian got back down on one knee. He told them it would be a deal that kept them alive, off death row and perhaps an assignment to a low security prison. He told them they would go to jail and would serve some significant time but they would stay alive.

The two looked at each other then asked what Ian wanted to know.

Ian told them he wanted the name of the top guy.

They both whispered the name Bradley Peterson.

Ian said thank you and stood up. He looked over at one of the agents and told him to read them their rights and stay with them in the ambulances. Guard them well and keep them alive and arrange lawyers for them.

One of the highway patrol officers asked what to do with Eduardo and Manuel.

Matt responded that the two should be taken back to the station and put back into the holding cell. He would deal with them at a later time.

Matt and Mike approached Ian. They wanted to know the name that the two policemen had given him.

Ian watched Matt as he gave out the name of Bradley Peterson.

Matt was surprised and said so. He commented that Bradley was second in command and that he was considered next in line to take over the sheriff's office.

Matt said he would give Bill a call and tell him to isolate Bradley and not let him destroy any records. Damn this is not going to be pretty Matt continued.

Ian was ready for the killing blow.

He suggested they all go to Bill's office and confront Bradley together. Ian made a call to his help number and requested a quick rundown on the finances of Bradley Peterson.

As the three arrived at the city police station, Ian received a call back on the finances for Bradley. Bradley was living very well for someone making one hundred thousand dollars a year. So far there seemed to be no indication of anything unusual in his bank accounts. They were not sure where he had gotten the money for a the very high-level life style he was living.

Ian told the group to check for transactions with any offshore account.

Bradley was sitting in Bob's office when the three walked in. Bob immediately commented that the request he had fulfilled was very unusual and he hoped there was a very good reason.

Ian looked at Bradley and formally put him under arrest for conspiracy against the US government.

There was silence in the room.

Ian was acting as if the case was clear and complete. He went on to list the fact that Bradley had aided and abetted the crossing of thousands of illegal aliens. It was most likely that he would be indicted for the deaths of more than thirty people found in the back of a panel truck, perhaps both trucks. He informed Bradley that he had been identified by two of his participating members who had turned state's evidence.

He asked Bradley what he had to say?

Bradley replied that the charges were preposterous. He refused to say anything until his lawyer was present.

That's fine, the FBI is already in the process of confiscating your computer and all your records, your secretary's computer and records, your associate's computers, and records. They have also entered your home and secured your home computer and any records you had there.

The FBI has also moved to freeze all your offshore bank accounts.

Your cooperation would be useful, but I prefer you refuse so that you get the death penalty, Ian continued as he leaned in almost nose to nose to Bradley.

Ian did not have most of the information he had just rattled off but he was in the mood to play poker and go for the winning hand via a bluff.

Bradley stood up and said he would consult with his lawyer and got up to leave.

Ian blocked his way and asked whether he had understood that he was under arrest and that his lawyer would need to come to him. Meanwhile he would cool his heals behind bars.

Ian turned to the two police officers standing in the room and told them to handcuff Bradley and read him his rights. The two looked at each other and finally one of them took his handcuffs and put them on Bradley. The other read Bradly his Miranda rights.

Ian turned to Bill and asked him if any of his officers had left early today. Whoever left is probably one of the guys working in dispatch. Ian went on to conjecture that there would be four or five individuals involved.

Ian's phone rang, and he held up his hand to stop the two police officers that were escorting Bradley out.

He went into an excited conversation and commented how much easier it was going to be to wrap up the investigation. He went on to thank the person on the line for making the connection to the offshore accounts happen so quickly. Ian instructed the person online to contact Mike Lancaster in the Phoenix office as soon as the bank accounts were secured.

Everyone in the room heard Ian's end of the conversation. The person on the other end wondered what was going on. He had been ready to tell Ian that it would take a while to identify and track down the offshore accounts.

Ian went on to comment how much easier it was going to be having made the link to the offshore accounts. Looking directly at Bradley he commented that it would have been smarter to use different offshore banks.

Ian walked over to Bradley and put his lips close to his ear and whispered, "if you don't talk, you won't live to see morning. I am an assassin sent to eliminate any obstacle to the resolution to this problem and I have just been cleared to assassinate you. If you talk you live."

Ian then pulled away only far enough to stare directly into Bradley's eyes. Then he turned and sat on the edge of Bob's desk.

Ian asked Bradley if he had anything to say.

"Alright, I am involved but Sam Henderson has been the mastermind of the operation. I provided a shield for the operation," Bradley confessed.

Ian was pleased with Bradley's reaction. Ian's threat had been real.

Ian turned to Mike and asked him to have a couple of his agents document Bradley's confession. They were to take down everything he knew about the operation and its finances. Have the remainder of those involved in the operation picked up.

Mike commented that the offshore bank link had really been found very fast. He had never heard of being able to track money so fast.

Once Bradley was out of the room, Ian let everyone know that the call had been to inform him that it would take a couple of days to a few weeks to track the accounts and that it would probably be impossible to tell where in the US the funds were coming from or going to. They needed more information from this end.

Everyone in the room agreed with Mike that it was one hell of a bluff. They all agreed that Ian was barred from their Saturday poker games.

Ian let that stand. He knew that it was his death threat that had tipped the scale.

He looked around and commented that they were almost done. When asked what remained, Ian pointed out that someone in Homeland Security had to be involved. The successes of the crossings were not an accident. The person or persons involved were as guilty of the deaths of two truckloads of people as the driver and those arranging the border crossings.

5 *A Short Ride*

6 Securing the Border

Art sipped on his Black Russian watching his young bikini clad companion diving, swimming across the pool then walking sexily back to the low diving board and doing it again. She was on her third round, and he was on his third drink. He figured that they were both about to change what they were doing. He knew that she would stretch out on a beach towel and spend most of the afternoon working on her tan. He was going to go into his office and work on finding the next weak person that he would recruit to help him in making sure his clients had a way to smuggle their clientele into the US.

He knew that he was living the high life, but he wished he could be doing so in New York City versus in Mexico City. He had fond memories of his early years in the Bronx. He still had many friends in the mafia's family business.

He unfortunately was a wanted man there. He had disciplined one of his collection clients a little too severely and had killed him. He had fled the state and later the country.

His boss in New York had put him in contact with one of the top lieutenants of the Sinaloa cartel. That introduction had opened the door to a relationship that had enriched him beyond his expectations. From the start he had been given access to the money that let him bribe and corrupt the protectors of the realm while at the same time he received a rewarding cash flow into his bank account.

It was not long before he was able to buy the home where he had now lived for several years. They had been good years that saw him make friends with many of the cartel's members. He was generous with his parties but kept them low key, which pleased the cartel leaders.

He got a monthly percentage of the money made by smuggling people north into the US. He never questioned the amount or even kept track of it. He focused on making sure that the crossings were facilitated and kept open as agreed to.

His mother, bless her soul, always told him that he would be successful, but he was sure that she would be surprised that his success would be in Mexico and not in New York City. She had always encouraged him and told him he would be as good as his father. He knew that he currently was about ten times as successful as his father had ever been. He had more money and more influence than his father had ever had.

Today he was reviewing the situation along the border. He had one reluctant player that was reacting to the news of the people that had died in the transport that had been abandoned in the middle of the desert. He personally had put out his feelers to see if the two drivers could be identified and eliminated. He had been reassured by his cartel contacts that it was in the works and only a matter of a very short time. He knew that the kind of news coverage that truck was getting was very bad for business. It made everyone un happy.

The word was out that drivers should know that the cartel would take care of them even if they were arrested.

He needed to do some repair work with the folks in the US border patrol that he had under his wing. He booked his flights and got ready for his very early morning flight.

He left from Mexico City at six in the morning and by noon he was in his favorite restaurant in Nogales for lunch. He sat enjoying his steak as he thought through how he was going to handle the situation.

He had gotten the hint of a problem from the scheduler, who he thought of as a pompous ass but who was easy to manage because he was in it for the money.

The potential problem was with the person that he actually liked but who was too emotionally connected to the plight of those trying to get into the US. The deaths of the people in that deserted truck had put him over the edge. His personal guilt was weighing heavily on him.

Art figured that he would need to use the threat of bodily harm to keep him in line. He would offer money as well, but he figured that money alone would not work. He decided that a missing bodily part of the loss of an eye would be the threat he would use.

Once lunch was over, he called for his driver who he used when making the trip. It was a short drive to Sasabe.

Sasabe, in Arizona was the actual location where he made contact with his border patrol people. He had purchased and had the interior of an old home there remodeled. It was literally next door to the bar where he connected with his border patrol people. He used a fake passport to cross over and after getting situated in his house he would walk over to the bar where he usually had dinner and watched some sports show until his contacts came in.

The young women, there were usually only a couple, appeared to be of Mexican or Indian heritage and usually approached the few young men that came in for drinks. He had come to recognize several of them and always bought them a drink.

He had made the trip because his drone operator had disobeyed a requested diversion and had cost them the crossing of a group of paying customers. He needed to get him back in line because he had to get that group across and on their way.

He was now also looking to activate his back up that he had been paying for more than a year. The cost of a backup was minimal, and he considered it a drop in the money bucket. He did not want to have two people active in the same location. He hoped to rectify the situation and hoped that the backup might get a change of assignment to some other location along the border.

He was nursing, a white Russian, when, Josh, his drone operator came in. He knew he was facing a person who had a very guilty conscious when the drink he chose was a plain sparkling water, when in the past it had always been a Margherita, no salt.

He listened as Josh spilled out his heart-felt sorrow about the truck load of people that had died such an inhumane death in the back of that truck in the desert. He confessed that the scene of the mother holding her two children to her breast was incised into his brain. He could not get it out of his mind and every day and night he saw it.

Art sympathized and said he understood the anguish. He felt bad for the people in that truck but for him it was due to two drivers who had abandoned their post. A sorry state of affairs but so was life. He then put down the hammer and threatened Josh with bodily harm if he ever broke his promise of doing as asked. He waited a moment and then offered the honey with a fifteen percent raise in the reward.

Josh shook his head, took a long drink and agreed to do as instructed. He thanked Art for the increase in the money but reminded him that he did not take the money but was having it sent to several charities and asked him to make sure they all got an even increase.

That reminded Art why Josh was one of his favorite people that he had corrupted. He thought of Josh as an ethically corrupted person. He nodded and said that he would see that the increase would be evenly distributed.

A day later he had a similar meeting with Ethan, the schedular for the patrol dog team. Ethan was his pompous self. Art thanked him for his heads-up warning and rewarded him with a five percent reward increase and told him to keep up the good work. He had contemplated not giving him anything but had decided against that. It was business and he let the percentage amount reflect his personal taste or distaste for the individual.

The next day he left and returned to his home in Mexico City.

7 The Scheduler

Ethan watched as Bradely met two men who arrived just before noon and after a brief conversation lead them into the building. He made it a point to walk out and go past the three and say good morning. The older white-haired person was dressed casually whereas the younger one looked like he was formally dress to impress someone who would decide whether to hire him. He stopped long enough to watch them go into Bradley's office. He wondered what was going on. The next day was scheduled for the crossing of the next group of border crossers. He hoped that it had nothing to do with that. He did not need his smoothly organized world to be disrupted.

He figured he was one of the luckiest guys in the world. He had grown up in one of the most beautiful areas in the US and seen what he considered the five wonders of the world all in the state where he had been raised.

In his youth he had walked the same trail as Lewis and Clark and had white water rafted there.

He had visited the Little Big Horn where the Battle of Little Bighorn was fought and where Custer died fighting several thousand Lakota, Cheyenne, and Arapaho warriors. He figured he was smarter than Custer and he would have defeated the Indians.

He and his parents had hiked through the Bighorn area and had been lucky enough to spot three Bighorn sheep. He had run toward them, and they had taken several leaps and run away.

As a scout he had taken many hikes through the Montana Rockies. Hikes that he figured were some of the best hiking in the world.

One vacation was spent in Glacier National Park hiking, camping and swimming in one of the coldest lakes he could remember. He had continued the swimming even though he came out blue each time.

In college he met, dated and married a beautiful woman and now had a family of four with one girl and one boy. His wife was a great cook and great at getting the family involved in the community.

He had become an ordained Evangelical minister and currently presided over a congregation of three hundred people. He really enjoyed delivering the sermons and watching the perishers kneeling down in front of him.

What he considered his one failing was his inability to find a job that fit his status. He had interviewed with all the large financial companies as well as the prestigious banks. He failed to understand why he had not received any offers.

The one offer he did receive came from the US border patrol organization with which he had interviewed on a lark.

His current role as a team scheduler for the border guards and their dogs was challenging but he knew that it was well below his true potential. He should be somewhere several levels above the position of his current boss, Bradley.

He felt great about his finances and was sure they were in great shape.

He had his government salary that came in just above six figures.

Surprisingly his salary for being the primary minister in his church was almost equal to the government salary. He had not realized that ministers made as much as they did.

He had been recruited by some Mexican cartel to adjust the border guard schedule to create holes in the coverage allowing the coyote guides to bring groups of people into the US without having to face the security patrols. The income from it was variable since he got paid for each group that made it through. There had been several months where that income was well above the sum of his other two incomes.

He justified that part of his behavior and correlated it to his role as minister to improving the life of the people that got into the US and besides it didn't hurt anyone.

Until recently everything along the border worked like clockwork. The hiccup had been the group of people that had died locked in the back of a truck out in the desert. He figured it was the cost of taking that kind of risk. They, not he had made that choice, so his conscience was clear.

He became aware that there was another person that was very emotionally affected by that situation. He had called the tip line that his cartel handler had given him and let him know about the situation. He didn't want some bleeding heart to ruining a great thing.

He figured that at the upcoming meeting with his handler he would get recognized for tipping him off and would likely get a hefty reward.

Meanwhile he made sure to adjust the scheduling and placement of the key ground teams so that a clear corridor was available to get people across the border at the designated times.

He thought about the meeting going on in Bradley's office and felt sure that none of them would have a clue how the border crossers were getting across the border. He figured that none of them were that smart.

It was not complex, but it was invisible unless someone was able to correlate all the times and the placement of the border guard teams.

He was sure his life was set and the only thing he had to worry about was figuring out how to get promoted to the right level.

8 Drone Operator

It all started one evening as he sat watching the Arizona Diamondbacks at the sports bar. Trey was approached by a man that introduced himself as Sam.

Sam had done his homework and knew Trey was sympathetic to the plight of the border crossers. He proposed a working relationship that offered a little extra money and a lot of personal satisfaction of helping people get to their dream. All he had to do was to misdirect the border patrol he was guiding. It would only take a few minutes, and no one would ever know. He pointed out that those entering the US were all fleeing from some bad people and were trying to better their lives.

The statement, "no one would ever know" alarmed Trey. How did Sam know so much about him? Trey replied that he would think about it.

A few weeks went by, and Trey had almost forgotten about the offer. Then he was on duty as a group of crossers refused to stop when confronted by the border guards.

They scattered and began to run and one of the guards pull out his gun and began to fire. Two to the crossers were hit. One was just wounded in the leg but a young boy in his early teens died on the scene.

Trey had watched the entire confrontation from his drone camera.

That incident made up his mind that he wanted to help the border crossers.

That weekend Sam again made contact with him at the sports bar.

Since that time, Trey had been aiding in the crossings by miss-positioning the guards.

This had been several years ago, and the operation ran smoothly and Trey felt that he was actually doing good.

Then he saw the news report about the dead border crossers piled in the back of a panel truck. He vowed he would not misdirect the border guards again. He knew that most border crossers who were trying for a better life in the US would be sent back. Those who truly were seeking asylum in fear of their lives would be processed and get their day in court.

He had played god and at least fifty people were dead.

He was not in it for the money and did not even bring money up when he was recruited. When finally asked about money, he inquired about the amount. It was to be two thousand a month. Trey agreed that is was significant, but he personally did not need or want it.

Trey pushed a piece of paper across the table to Sam. There were three organizations on it: Red Cross Relief Fund, United Appeal, and Catholic Social Services. He bargained for more by asking that each organization get a thousand dollars each month and that a confirmation post card be sent to him.

Sam readily agreed to the arrangement. He would have paid double that amount if he had been asked.

The redirecting went on smoothly until the abandoned truck with all the bodies had made the news. Trey was shocked and wondered if he had contributed to the deaths of the people. In his mind he was sure that he had.

Two trucks abandoned in the middle of the desert. The sun making the metal skin of the panel truck's metal exterior hot enough to fry an egg. People abandoned to die in the suffocating oven like heat. Humans so desperate that they broke their bodies against the backdoors in an attempt to break out. Humans so desperate that their fingernails ripped out in their attempt to claw their way out.

These were constant elements of Trey's nightmares. But the scene of the two dead children being lovingly held to their mother's dead chest played in both his sleep and daylight cycles. He could not shake the vision and the knowledge that he was part of putting those people through the hell of their last few hours of their lives.

Trey knew he was on the verge of a mental breakdown. He loathed himself. He had succumbed to the lure of easy money for helping those poor border crossers. He truly was sympathetic to their cause. He now believed he had made a deal with the devil. He had sold his soul for a small bag of gold. He could not forgive himself.

He went to the bar several times hoping to make contact with Sam. But it never happened.

The reality of his situation hit Trey hard. He took vacation and drank himself into a stupor for two weeks.

He vowed he would not misdirect the border guards again.

He had played god and at least fifty people were dead.

Trey returned to work and followed his conscious for the following week. Then the signal for misdirection came into him.

He ignored it and the group coming across was apprehended.

He got a call at his home that night. He was told that if he missed the next misdirection signal, he would lose the sight of his left eye and the loss of one finger. If he did as he was told, he would get a ten percent bonus for each event.

Trey immediately understood that he was indeed working for the devil, and he was in a trap. He would suffer dearly for not following orders.

He wrote down the phone number from which the threat had been made. He did not know how to trace it to a source but a friend of his probably could.

Trey imagined finding the culprit and taking some sort of action to eliminate him.

He realized immediately that he did not have the courage to follow through. He knew he was being threatened by one of the cartels in Mexico.

He could accept them killing him. He deserved being killed. He could not imagine or accept the torture they were threatening.

Two days later he again got the signal to misdirect a specific border security team.

Trey diverted the border guards just to the west of where the crossing was to occur. The truck was parked only a mile from the boarder in a small ravine. It was visible from the air but the team on the ground did not see it as they passed only a few hundred yards away.

Trey complied but it came to him that someone else was also on the take. Each time the misdirection was targeted at a specific team and at a specific time. He had never thought about this key fact. Someone else in the organization who knew the schedule and location of the security teams had to be involved.

Trey began keeping track of which schedulers were on duty on the days he got the misdirection signal.

Again, Trey came to the realization that when he figured out who it was, he was not sure what he would do.

He wondered if he could leave the region and not be found.

A few days later the FBI toured the drone control facility. Trey listened as the supervisor explained the interaction of the drone operators with the various border patrol teams.

He figured his days were numbered. It was clear to him that the older FBI agent was in charge. He listened intently and asked the kind of questions that made it clear he understood how easily it would be for a drone operator to misdirect the action on the ground.

Trey thought about the old saying about being between a rock and a hard place. He figured he was between hell and if extremely lucky a long term in jail if he could avoid a death sentence.

At this point jail seemed to be the safest place to be. Trey thought about his complicity and the thought of a death sentence silenced him.

Trey succumbed to drinking himself asleep each night. He awakened in the morning to his nightmares. His work life was miserable. He barely ate. He was a mess.

Trey knew that the noose around his neck was tightening. He did not know how much longer he could take his self-inflicted pressure.

He made a point of documenting everything he knew about the situation.

He had made up his mind. He was going to take his own life. It was the only pain free way to escape the situation he was in.

He wondered if his parents would understand. He was their only child. He took the time to write them a letter explaining his situation and said he loved them and hoped they would forgive him.

All that remained was to work up the courage to do it and he knew that deep inside he was a coward.

He was at work and in the process of again misdirecting a field team of border guards when he again observed the FBI agent come into the Border Security office.

Trey immediately knew what he was going to do.

First, he walked over to the shredder and put in the suicide letter to his parents.

9 Closure

*T*he several-hour ride to the Homeland Security offices somewhere out in the desert provided Mike and Ian time to talk.

Mike asked what Ian had whispered to Bradley to get him to confess so fast.

Ian shared that he had reminded Bradley that it was going to be a long night and he was not going to have to give up his belt or tie, but much could happen to him before the sun came up. Bradley's imagination did the rest. Ian left out the part where he told Bradley he was the assassin sent out to kill whoever was behind the truck incident.

The drive through the bleak desert terrain of patches of tumble weeds, cactuses and some dry looking grasses seemed to compliment the stones, blowing dirt or maybe brown sand and a wide dead looking terrain. The sky was cloudless. Ian figured it was too hot for any moisture to rise and condense. He wondered when the last rain had been.

He was glad to let Mike do the driving since it gave him time to reflect.

He relaxed and concentrated on how they would flush out the guilty party or parties at the Homeland office. Ian suspected that there was more than one person involved. He expected at least one person to be a drone operator. Such a person would be able to misguide the group personnel, so the border crossers could pass by, but timing was a key factor. That meant some one scheduling the teams on the ground was most likely to be involved.

They were to again meet with Tom Hemsley, the station supervisor. Ian hoped Tom was not involved. It would really be a bad situation if he were.

Tom was standing by to receive the FBI agents coming to meet with him. He had worked with Matt and Bill and had attended a cookout where his family and their families had shared a picnic table. Their kids had played and now his kids were always asking when there was going to be another police picnic in Phoenix. He had met Mike the FBI regional leader at that picnic.

On the other hand, the FBI agent that was currently helping Mike, scared the bejesus out of him. His penetrating gaze and his direct and rather aggressive manner made Tom nervous. He knew it would not be a good idea to get in his way.

Tom had one of his crew scouting for an incoming car. He did not want any surprises. He would meet the two in the parking lot before bringing them into the building. Once they entered everyone in the building would know and wonder why the two had come back again.

Ian saw the Homeland Security agent riding an RTV alongside of the highway. He figured him for a scout out verifying the incoming traffic.

Ian let Mike know that Tom knew that they were arriving. And it appeared that he was nervous about their arrival.

Mike conjectured that perhaps they should have told him more about their purpose in coming. It would have been easier if they could totally count on him and his immediate reports and got their help.

Ian pointed out the situation they had just experienced. What would have happened in their interactions at the sheriff's office if Bob had shared any information with Bradley.

Mike looked at Ian and decided never to play poker or chess with him. He knew Ian would not cheat. He would just figure out how to beat you. It was clear to Mike that Herman Lunquist never left anything to chance.

Mike agreed with him. His personal connection with Tom and his family gave him confidence that Tom was in the clear.

He did not know how but he was confident that Herman would find the guilty.

Ian saw Tom standing under the building entrance canopy on the edge of the parking lot. Tom pointed to an empty parking space almost directly in front of the canopy. Matt parked in the space to which Tom pointed.

Tom greeted Mike with a handshake and a man hug. Ian liked him for doing that. Ian was a hugger with people he knew.

Tom gave Ian a formal and firm handshake.

Before escorting them in, Tom wanted to know why the FBI was back and in such a cryptic fashion.

It took all his inner strength and control, but he glanced at Mike and then focused on Herman.

Ian smiled. Tom's actions made it clear to him that Tom stood by his people. He was a protector. He would be devastated if one of them were involved in helping the smugglers to smuggle people across the border that he was sworn to patrol and enforce. This was going to be as hard on him as it had been on Bill

Ian quietly told Tom that one or more of his people were corrupt. He had come to determine who in the drone team was involved and who on the scheduling team was involved. Ian figured that the two positions would be the minimum number involved in the border crossing scheme.

He asked Tom if that was a problem.

Tom got angry and asked how the hell he was so sure any one of his people were involved.

Ian calmly replied that it was more than one and that it was the only explanation that fit the situation.

Mike decided to break the tension. He explained what had just transpired in Phoenix where the second in command of the police department had confessed to hiring the truck drivers and having the trucks rented.

Tom stood silently for a moment. Then he muttered, "Jesus this is going to play hell with our organization if some of our folks are involved. They are likely to get shot by their angry coworkers."

Ian pointed out that it was time for them to go in and figure out how to spot the perpetrators.

Tom nodded and led the way into the building and up to his office.

From his window desk on the second floor Trey saw the trio walking in. He knew the jig was up. He was glad. He walked over to the shredder and shredded the suicide letter he had delayed in sending to his parents.

He was going to turn himself in. He would not wait to be interrogated. He wasn't sure what the penalty was for what he had done but it couldn't be worse than the sleepless nights and continuous anguish that he was now experiencing. He figured it was one step above suicide.

He got up, walked to Tom's office where the three were meeting and knocked on the door.

Ian was surprised as Trey walked in and simply said that he was the one they were looking for. Someone turning themselves in had not been on Ian's list of how to find the perpetrator.

Ian stood up and asked Trey to take his seat. He turned so he could see Tom's reaction.

Ian asked Trey to explain why the FBI would be interested in him.

Trey held up a thumb drive and explained that he had documented all he knew about how the border crossings were managed. He explained that he periodically received a divert signal and the time and place of the diversion of the ground guard team to be diverted. Trey commented on the fact that he had come to the conclusion that one of the schedulers had to be involved.

Ian asked how long Trey had been doing this and how he had been recruited.

Trey said it was all detailed on this thumb drive.

Ian thanked Trey for the documentation but said he wanted to hear it in Trey's own words. He asked Tom to record Trey's confession. He asked Mike to read Trey his Miranda rights. He took the thumb drive and gave it to Mike.

Trey had tears in his eyes. It was hard for him to see. The flood of emotion was overwhelming him.

He began to cry.

Through his crying he explained that the vision of the dead mother holding her two dead children to her chest would be with him forever. If there was a hell, he said he was sure to go there. He was sure that truck had been one of the ones used when he had diverted the ground crew.

Ian looked at Tom and asked if there was a secure room where Trey could be put.

Ian wanted some time to review what was on the thumb drive, so they could determine their next steps.

Ian asked that Tom, Mike, and he together review the contents of the thumb drive.

After locking Trey in a secure room, Tom plugged the thumb drive into his computer and opened the only file that was on it.

It was clear that Trey had provided a detailed account of his recruitment. He had provided the time and dates of all the diversions. Trey had come to the realization that a person in scheduling had to also be involved and had narrowed it down to two people.

Ian scanned all the information. He came to a much more startling theory.

Trey had not done it for the money, but the scheduler most probably had done it for money. The cartels had billions of dollars with which to work. Sam, or whatever his real name was, had most probably recruited multiple people. Why stop at one. There was money to be made. He would want to have backups. He would recruit as many people as possible.

Ian realized that there were probably sleeper candidates that were ready to step in when he arrested those people currently involved.

He looked at Tom and could see that he was angry about what was transpiring. Ian knew that if he were in Tom's position, he would be wondering who else was on the take. This was probably Tom's most dreaded situation.

Tom personally knew one of the two, Ethan, as a true family man and an upstanding member of his church. He picked Josh as the most likely one to be recruited. He was the one that was forever coming up with an excuse for being late to work and he dressed in a slovenly manner.

The selection made little sense to Ian. He had known too many family men who had let their ego and desire for personal goods sell out their families.

Ian walked out of the office and put in a call to his support team. He asked them to check out the two schedulers. He asked them to especially look at the bank accounts and spending habit changes. They were also to look through the background clearance checks and see if there were any gaps in the information.

He returned and asked Tom to bring in the person he suspected.

A young looking, man that probably got carded every time he ordered a drink came through the door. Ian stepped forward and shook hands with Josh. He appeared to be sixteen but was probably in his early thirties. He sported a scraggly beard and a head of hair that was greased and made into spikes. What Ian took to be a punk head.

It was clear that Tom did not especially like Josh and that Josh knew this and probably presented himself in the way he did as a way to irritate Tom.

Almost instantly Ian figured it was the family man that would be the culprit. Josh seemed too confident and together to be the one.

Ian also concluded that Tom was a biased judge of character.

Mike watched Ian's interactions with Josh. Ian pressed him on how he scheduled his teams. He pressed him hard about the timing and placement of the teams and who he shared this information with.

Ian then probed into Josh's personal life. Was he single? Yes, did he have a girlfriend? How often did he go out? Where did they go out? Was he getting laid?

Josh remained cool and collected. He calmly answered Ian's questions and even joked with Ian about his poor love life and the fact that there was no place to go in this forsaken part of the world. He did not seem disturbed. He laughed at the last question and answered, "not enough."

Ian thanked Josh for answering his questions and made a point that there would be a follow-up the following day.

As Josh was leaving, he invited Ian for a drink if he was staying in town that evening.

Ian turned to Tom and asked him to bring in Ethan for his interview.

Mike came to the conclusion that Ethan was in for a really thorough grilling. It was clear to him that Josh had passed the grilling he had undergone, with flying colors.

Ethan reminded Mike of Bradley who had been confident that he was above suspicion.

Ian asked similar questions to what he had asked Josh. The answers Ethan gave were always logical and often supported with examples of his family and church life. He put on the air of a loving father that focused on his family life.

Ian decided it was time to use the one threat that he knew would work.

Ian leaned in close to Ethan's ear. He whispered a curse, "you god damn soulless son of a bitch. I have your offshore bank account number and the times you refilled your account. I know exactly when you were recruited. I am not an FBI agent. The government does not desire to be embarrassed and has sent me out to eliminate anyone who does not confess to their deeds. You have to the count of twenty and then I leave and tonight you die."

Tom was looking at Mike. He mouthed, "What is he saying?"

Mike just shrugged and tilted his head. He had the gist but had no clue as to the actual words. He watched as Ethan's face went white. To Mike this was the face of someone who was guilty.

Ian stepped back. Ethan put his elbows on his knees and leaned his face into his cupped hands. It was clear that he was crying.

Ian counted slowly to twenty. When he said twenty out loud, Ethan fell to his knees and cried out, "Please forgive me. I just wanted to be a better provider for my family."

Tom looked at Herman with newfound respect. He told Ethan it was not their role to forgive. He would be tried for his misdeeds. A judge and jury would decide his fate.

Ian asked Mike to read Ethan his rights. He looked at Tom who was looking a little pale and appeared to be in a state of shock.

Ian knew that if Tom was kept employed, he was now in line for reassignment to the most remote location possible.

Ian asked that Trey and Ethan be held in custody. He and Matt would transport both Ethan and Trey to Phoenix where they would be arraigned.

Ian knew the follow-up investigations would go on for a long time. He looked at Mike and commented that he would have his hands full for the foreseeable future. He was sure that his coming promotion would help.

The next day, the drive to Phoenix was eerily quiet. Ian was sitting in the back seat with Ethan who had his handcuffed hands on his lap.

Trey sat quietly in the right front seat looking out the window. It was clear that he had found whatever peace he would have for the rest of his life. He seemed calm. Ian figured confession had freed his soul.

Ethan on the other hand went from whimpering to full sobs. He was still wrestling with his demons. Ian would make sure he was put on suicide watch.

The expanse of the desert seemed to go on forever until it met the black and dark green of the Rockies. The blue of the cloudless sky seemed appealing until the heat of the day hit your face.

Ian decided the best thing for him to do was to doze lightly. Mike seemed to be fully concentrating on his driving. There was silence in the car.

Mike had called ahead and made arrangements with Bill to have space available for the two they were bringing in. He also let him know that each had obtained the services of a lawyer. The lawyers were going to meet their clients the next day. The two would be arraigned on Friday.

Mike planned to hold a news conference in the morning. He asked Herman to take the lead.

Ian declined. He led Mike to believe that it would ruin his future in solving cases like the one they had just solved together.

Mike found this a little hard to believe but he knew the news conference to share the success would certainly help his career. He remembered Herman asking him what he hoped for. Mike knew solving this case would certainly lead to a promotion. He wondered how it would affect Herman.

At breakfast Bill and Matt asked why Herman was not taking part in the press conference.

Mike made the point that publicity would make it harder for him to be effective in the future.

Matt looked at Ian and quietly mouth the work "bullshit".

Ian smiled and simply said that the dancing in the spotlight was Mike's job. He said his job was done and it was time for him to move on. He made the point that there were many other problems that still need to be solved.

Bill looked at Ian as he took a sip of his coffee. He made the comment that he did not believe Ian worked for the FBI.

"Let's just say I am called on to solve the problems that are defying solution in a normal manner. I work for whoever needs my help" Ian replied. I am a problem solver.

"Well, whoever you may be, thanks for getting to the bottom of this situation. I would have never believed anyone in my organization would have been involved in such a scheme. I will forever be in your debt," Bill said from his side of the table.

"Well, I am on the way home and that is always a treat. My wife is the best cook in the world," Ian said as he got up.

He was on the way to meet a helicopter at Montezuma Castle National Monument. It would take him all the way home and to the arms of his lovely Lesley.

"I thought he was single," Ian heard Matt say to Bill as he walked out.

Ian smiled. He had never discussed his personal life with anyone. They had reached their own conclusion.

The End

Preview: Of Rhinos and Horns

1 Daimler-End of the Road

Their escape from the pirates was the most dramatic event in Maurice's and Ted's lives. Matt's handling of the battle was a lesson in preparation and in how to totally devastate your opponent. Only a few of the twenty some attack pirate boats disappeared in what seemed to be a crater created by the explosion of every boat.

Then the command ship attacked and once again it seemed that they were going to be captured by a ship armed with a deck cannon that put a shell on each side of the Lazy Lady.

Then Maurice watched as Matt pressed a button and the entire front end of the giant on coming ship blew up as if it had been hit by some unseen rocket.

She rejoiced when Matt asked Ted to hoist the main sail and the jib, and she felt the Lazy Lady come to life and seemingly leap forward in joy.

They sailed into Cape Town where Matt left them.

A short time after they docked Matt left them to return to the US.

She and Ted sailed the Lazy Lady out of Cape Town to continue on their around the world sailing tour. They sailed north along the coast of Africa. They stopped at almost every port for a day so that they could enjoy the various historic sites but mostly because it allowed them to enjoy the wide variety of dishes and did not have to cook or clean. This took them several months and then before entering the Med, they returned to the US to celebrate the births of grandchildren and spend a few days with the new children.

They were known to the family as the grandparents that sailed the world. Maurice accepted the title with pride and offered to pay the airfare for any family member that desired to join them on the Lazy Lady.

After being away for more than a month they returned to the Lazy Lady that they had come to considered home. Each time they returned they would talk about the time they were saved by Matt from being taken hostage by the Pirates of the coast of East Africa. They would laugh at the fact that they had never asked and now did not know his last name. They would have loved dearly to communicate with him and share the highlights of their journey.

They sailed into the Mediterranean and did a counter clockwise tour. They stopped in Algiers, Tunis, Tripoli and when four months later they got to Alexandria, they once again flew back to the US to celebrate Thanksgiving. After enjoying the family and all their grandchildren they decided to stay for Christmas. This allowed them to play Santa parents and spoil their brewed of grandchildren.

On their return they continued on and went to see Jerusalem where they spent more than a week visiting all the religious sites.

They then sailed to Beirut and from there sailed to Cyprus. They stopped briefly in Antalya, Turkey to rejuvenate and get the Lazy Lady refreshed.

Then it was on to Athens where they spent a week visiting all the historic sites that they had studied in high school and college.

Then up northward up eastern side of the Adriatic Sea with brief stops in several of sea ports. The longest stay was at the very northern part when they reached Venice. They toured Venice for a week and then sailed nonstop to Catania, Sicily before going on to Naples.

There they once again left the Lazy Lady while they flew home for several grandchildren's graduations from high school and college. This was only a brief visit, and, on their return, they sailed to Fiumicino where they anchored for a week as they visited Rome. Their next stop was Livorno where they stopped so they could take a road trip to Florence.

The sailing continue for the rest of the year as the two visited Genoa, Nice, Marseille Barcelona and Valencia.

They left the Mediterranean and sailed north and stopped in Lisbon.

From there they sailed straight to Dublin where they stayed for more than a month to tour Ireland. It was during this period that they once again flew back to the states.

They continued their sailing for yet two more years and would spend time visiting many of the cities in the UK, spent a month in Amsterdam and then took a boat tour down the Rhine to Switzerland and back.

They chuckled when they lined the Lazy Lady with a row of potted flowers.

They waited until summer to sail into the Bering Sea and hit many of the ports like Helsinki, Stockholm and Copenhagen.

Their last stop on the way back to the States was Edinburgh where they spent several weeks relaxing and touring the countryside.

Once they made New York they took another family break and flew back to LA to celebrate in Pasadena where the majority of the family now lived.

After a few weeks they flew back to the Lazy lady.

Once they returned to the Lazy Lady, it took them another five years to bring her through the Panama canal and up the coast of Baja California. They finally docked the Lazy Lady and arranged for her complete overhaul.

The Lazy Lady was taken out of the water and literally refurbished and restored to the point where she was once again like new. Her engine and the appliance were all replaced.

They then sailed on her for almost another ten years and then when they could no longer do so on their own. They arranged to once again refurbish the Lazy Lady.

It was during this last time of renewing the Lazy Lady that after checking with their sons, they decided that the person who had rescued them from the pirates off the coast of Africa should be the new owner of the yacht that he had saved from the pirates.

Maurice had looked ahead and every year for the last five years she had held a family goodbye party. She had done much of the baking and preparation for the first party but for the other four years had the party catered. These parties let everyone involved deal with the fact that there was an end point to everyone's journey.

Shortly after, both went into Hospice care where they shared the same apartment for what they knew would be their final journey together. They had settled all their accounts and knew that they had shared a wonderous life together.

Their two sons who were now nearing their own retirement and their children who were now all grown adults themselves and who had children all stopped by to say their goodbyes.

Their wealth was significant but not exceedingly huge, most of their estate was in the business that they had passed on to their sons. However, there was still a sizeable amount that was in trust with specific instructions of how that was to be handled.

The biggest challenge that they had worked through was how to pass the Lazy Lady on to the one person who they agreed should be the one to inherit it.

They only knew him as Matt, so they put an advertisement in the personal section of several newspapers in major cities across the US that simply gave their names and the fact that they had been saved from being captured by pirates by someone sent to save them. They wanted to reward that person and needed to get in contact with him to make sure he accepted the ownership of the Lazy Lady.

They kept that Ad active for more than three years and were giving up hope when they received the call that they had waited for what to them seemed to be an eternity. They learned the name of the person they would pass the Lazy Lady to. It was less than a year later that they both took that name with them to eternity when within a month of each other they passed away.

The person who had contacted them was Ian's handler. He had met with Maurice's and Ted's lawyer and had made all the legal arrangements for the transfer.

Not a month later he was online with Ian letting him know of their passing and the fact that they had left him the Lazy Lady as a measure of their gratitude.

The contact with Ian had more to do with a problem requiring his special touch than about the yacht. It had to do with a high stakes kidnapping that needed to be resolved. It needed the special touch of the Problem-Solver.

Ian knew immediately that he would put the Lazy Lady to work as part of the solution that he had in mind.

2: Rise to Power

General Ingraditi was frustrated by the situation of the current Army Command. He controlled much of the country, but his two longtime nemesis seemed to currently have the upper hand. For years he had been hounded by General Mumbada and his longtime friend General Wesbow who controlled about forty percent of the country. The two were inseparable and were able to fend off his many attempts to derail them and take complete control of the army.

He was upset with the support they were given by a group of wealthy businessmen that had great influence with the general assembly. It was a delicate situation that he knew he would win in the near future when it came to head that very likely might be a bloody confrontation.

He had the loyalty of the larger part of the army but that only meant that he could defend the territory he currently controlled and keep his adversaries at bay.

He knew that the richest part of Nairobi was in the hands of General Mumbada and the part of the army that had his loyalty. As long as that was the case, he would have to put up with General Mumbada.

As General Ingraditi lamented, needing to put up with his adversary, General Mumbada, followed by his longtime friend, Vice General Wesbow walked slowly down the line of soldiers they were inspecting.

The last two soldiers were dressed in very expensive black suits that had been awarded to them for their superior service to the army. The general lightly brushed the thousand-dollar suits and congratulated each of the soldiers for their superior service and shook their hands. He was sure that his reward-based recognition was loved by his army. He knew that they were loyal to him more than the parts of the army controlled by his superior.

He and General Wesbow were friends since their childhood when they were in grade school. At that time Kenya was still in the control of Great Briton and was known as British East Africa. The two of them were disturbed to see the British and European farmers prospering by growing coffee and tea on the rich Kenyan land while the general population was struggling to make ends meet. The two came to despise the inequity of the situation and throughout their younger years they and their friends played games where they rid the country of foreigners and became the leaders who took Kenya to higher power in the world.

He and Lionel Wesbow remained friends as they grew older. They had parents that pushed them to do well in school and later to get into the Army. The two went to and graduated from a school similar to the US army's West Point Academy.

He had the framed degree stating that Maurice Mumbada had graduated first in the class of 1976 proudly displayed on the wall of his office. He knew that Lionel had a similar degree that stated he had graduated second that he had hung in his office.

It was a time where the country's many clans and forty some differing languages kept the various clans apart from each other. In 1963 after facing internal rebellion, the British relinquished control and the following year Kenya became an independent nation.

Kiswahili became the common language. That was the language that the two had grown up with. They were fluent in English which put them in a great position as they made their way up the army ranks.

In the following years they focused on what it took to get ahead and made sure that both were at the right place at the right time. They were both rewarded with the promotions that they sought.

There was always the one person to whom they were both junior to and who seemed to be promoted just ahead of the two of them.

The two now in controlled of most of the western part of the country and wide strip that extended down to the Indian Ocean.

General Ingraditi, who they supposedly reported to controlled the eastern and northern part of Kenya.

Their reporting relationship with Ingraditi was frosty but they made sure that it would not reach the point of direct confrontation.

The area they controlled included Nairobi that was several million people strong and the entire area they controlled included sixty percent of the population.

They recognized that their main strength was the support of a group of wealthy businessmen that were prospering by having them look the other way to their across the border self-serving business dealings.

General Ingraditi controlled more territory and had to interface with four boundary countries whereas he only dealt with the politics of dealing with two border countries.

They felt certain that they had enough power that they could take control of the entire country, but it would put them at risk of a battle between the men loyal to them and those loyal to General Ingraditi. It would entail an internal battle that would not be good for them or the country. It was clear to them that it might increase their ability to add to the billions to what they already had in their Swiss bank accounts.

They decided they were in a strong position and should continue to wait to make their upward move when the opportunity presented itself.

General Ingraditi gave them the idea of how to increase the cash flow to their bank accounts. He periodically kidnapped some important business man and then demanded a ransom. When the ransom was paid the business man was released. The timing of the kidnappings varied but they were far enough apart that the public attention span waned, and another kidnapping did not alarm the population.

They liked that idea, but they planned to do the same on a grander scale. The opportunity to do so presented itself a few weeks after they had agreed to the ransom idea.

The Society of Geographic Exploration contacted General Mumbada and asked for his support for a four-member film crew that they wanted to send into the country to document the condition of the black rhino population. They were seeking his support so that the team would be able to safely travel around the various parks to photograph the rhinos in their natural habitat.

He and General Wesbow immediately set into motion a plan to kidnap the team and then demand five million dollars for the release of each film crew member.

A few months later when the film team arrived, they were met by a specially assigned army squad that was assigned to take them to a holding location until the ransom was paid. The kidnapping was a nonevent. A black van met the team as they exited the airport with all their equipment.

The driver and his companion helped load all the equipment and suitcases into the van and then drove to a destination outside of Nairobi where the team was to be held.

Soon after, General Mumbada learned that there was a nasty interaction with the female team leader when she insisted, they be taken to their hotel. He was told that she had a bruise that covered her right cheek where she had been backhanded. He asked for the soldiers name who had hit the leader and he also sent word that the film crew was to be treated well. He had them separated and locked in two separate rooms of the barracks where they were being held.

He and Lionel discussed how they would handle the four when the ransom was paid.

He publicly announced the film crew's abduction and said that the army was in pursuit of the kidnappers who were demanding a ransom of five million dollars per person for their safe release. He assured the news channels that the team would be found and rescued by his men.

General Ingraditi learned of the kidnapping as he listened to a news report. He was shocked by the amount of ransom that was being demanded. He was also sure that his two nemesis and strong competitors for control of the army were the ones behind the kidnapping.

He sent them a cryptic message stating, "it is not me so it must be something the two of you have cooked up. I am staying clear of it."

He was not staying clear. He set forth a plan that brought his army units closer to Nairobi in preparation of arresting both General Mumbada and General Wesbow. It seemed that the two were getting greedy and that they would no doubt think about gaining more power as well as more money.

General Mumbada and Wesbow were glad to get the message and figured that they had clear sailing and would soon be able to send a significant amount of money to their Swiss bank accounts.

They were disappointed when they news from The Society of Geographic Exploration saying that the US would not allow the organization to meet the ransom demands. This worried them but they figured it was just the first step in the ransom demand dance. They agreed that they should reiterate the ransom demand that threatened harm to the film crew if the demand was not met.

A few days later they received a reply to the ransom demand that asked how the payment should be delivered. The message was signed, Matthew Parker ransom settlement specialist.

They figured that the company had hired an outsider to deliver the ransom money.

They had never heard of a "ransom settlement specialist" but they were pleased that the ransom was to be paid. They hoped that this specialist would arrive at the airport with the ransom money where their men would quickly put this would be specialist out of business when they took control of the ransom money.

They organized a team to seize the ransom money. They had come to the conclusion that eliminating the film crew would make it easier for them to close out the kidnapping situation.

It was clear to them that their kidnapping case had grown roots and would yield the millions that they had hoped. They congratulated each other on having come up with such a lucrative idea.

They decided that a celebration outing was appropriate and visited the most expensive restaurant in Nairobi and celebrated their success.

The two would not have been celebrating if they had known who Mathew Parker was and how he solved the problems that he was assigned and the many years that he had successfully done so.

While they celebrated Mathew Parker was on his way to solve the problem they had created.

Thanks for reading this far;

To finish the previewed story

go to: https://www.remwriter95.net/

About the Author

Ronald E. Mueller
remwriter95@gmail.com

Ron grew up in what is now Flint River State Park in Southeast Iowa. The 170-year-old house Ron lived in is built into a hillside. It faces a 125-foot-high cliff towering over the little Flint River. The house and the land talked to him about; the passing of time, the struggle to conquer the land, the struggles people faced and the wonder of nature.

He climbed the cliffs, crawled into the caves, dove from the swimming rock, collected clams from the bottom of the pond, gigged and skinned frogs for their legs. He trapped muskrats for fur, hunted raccoon in the dead of night, and with only a stick hunted rabbits in the dead of winter.

His young life was outdoors, and nature tested him.

He walked to a one room stone schoolhouse uphill both ways. A stern but warm-hearted teacher, Mrs. Henry was instrumental in shaping his character as she shepherded him from the fourth to the eighth grade.

It was a great way to grow up.

Ron graduated from Burlington, High School, went to Vietnam in the Navy. He graduated from The University of South Florida with a master's degree in engineering, worked for thirty eight years for Procter and Gamble, traveled around the world thirty times.

He has remained happily married for more than fifty years. His daughter and his two sons are all successful and his three grandchildren have all graduated.

His wife has humored and supported him as he became a full time professional story teller.

He has come to realize that he is, what is known as, a Cozy writer. Excitement and adventure but little guts and gore. His heroine or hero suffer a little but live happily ever after.

His experiences inter-twined with snippets of fantasy lend themselves to the adventures he leads the reader through.

Books by the Author

Fiction Series
The Alex Evercrest Series
The River Front
The Girl on The Grill
Missing
Maggot
Racist
Votive Candles
Windy City
Country Road
Pool of Blood
Sins of the Daughter
Body Parts
The Skull Collector
The Vanishing
The Shadow Fighter
Moonshine
Grief's Trajectory
The Magic Touch
Northern Lights
Alex Evercrest Heroine
Alex Evercrest Collection Two
New Direction
A Family Affair
Disruption
Aftermath
The St. Lebuinnus Church Murder

A Brian O'Neil Novel
Hawaiian Phoenix
Moon Curser
Death Broker

The Problem Solver Series
Solutions
Drug Lords
Border Crosser
The Problem Solver Collection

The Taelo Series
The Early Years
The Golden Feather
Journey of Discovery
Dangerous Passage
Condor Clan Slingers
Circumvention
The Journey of Sages
Collection
Future Leaders Journey

A Taelo Story:
White Swan and Quiet Pheasant
The Child's Name
Floating Cloud
Quiet Rabbit
Busy Bee
Little Otter & Talking Wren
Broken Spear
Burley Bear & Meadow Flower
Taelo Story Collection

Science Fiction

The Savitar Series:
Journey's End
Savitar
Confluence
Savitar Series Collection

Bram Nielson Series
The Fold
The Message
Fold Wormhole
Negative Fold
Ripples in Time
Bram Nielson Collection

Single Science Fiction Books:
Current Past and Future
The Event
The Door
Viajante 7

118

https://www.remwriter95.net/

Published by: Around the World Publishing LLC.